The Island of
Serenity
Part 1

The Island of Esteem
Vol 2

'Le Morte d'Arthur'

By

Gary Edward Gedall
28 02 2018

Published by

From Words To Worlds

Images synthesized by Boris:
avasta.studio@gmail.com

Print Edition
ISBN: 2-940535-43-9
ISBN 13: 978-2-940535-43-9

By the same Author

Adventures with the Master

REMEMBER

The Island of Serenity, Pt 1 Destruction
   (Series – published or in preproduction)

Non Fiction -   (published or in preproduction)

The Zen approach to Low Impact Training and Sports

The Zen approach to Modern Living
    Vol 1 Fundamentals, Family & Friends
    Vol 2. Work, Rest & Play
    Vol 3 Life Cycle

Picturing the Mind:
    Vol 1   Basic Principals
    Vol 2   Fields within Fields
    Vol 3   Pathology, classical, traditional and
                   alternative healing methods

About the Author

Gary Edward Gedall is a state registered psychologist, psychotherapist, trained in Ericksonian hypnosis and EMDR.

Gary has ordinary and master's degrees in Psychology from the Universities of Geneva and Lausanne and an Honours Degree in Management Sciences from Aston University in the UK.

He has lived as an associate member of the Findhorn Spiritual Community, and has been a regular visitor to the Osho meditation centre in Puna, India. As part of his continuing quest into alternative beliefs and healing practices, he completed the three-year practical training, given by the Foundation for Shamanic Studies in 2012.

He has completed, in 2016 a professional, post graduate training; DAS, (Diploma of Advanced Studies), as a therapist using horses, (Equine Assisted Therapist)

Gary's hobbies are; writing, western riding and spoiling his children. He also, writes regularly for the Quora internet forum, (Quora writer of the year 2015 and 2018, 800,000 views, as of Feb. 2018).

Disclaimer:

The characters and events related in my books are a synthesis of all that I have seen and done, the people that I have met and their stories.

Hence, there are events and people that have echoes with real people and real events, however no character is taken purely from any one person and is in no way intended to depict any person, living or dead.

My books are not, in any way therapy books and are not meant to contradict or invalidate, any other vision of the human being or their psyche, nor any particular therapy.

Author's Notes

Self-esteem is quite a complex theme.
To accept, appreciate and love oneself in a healthy and balanced fashion is not an easy thing to accomplish.

We are all driven by our wants, needs and desires, (the 'id' in psychodynamic terms, or the 'child' in transactional analysis).

Yet, we all have some form of 'higher self' or critical functioning that has expectations of how we 'should' be, (the 'superego' or the 'parent').

And then we have the everyday thinking part, (the ego, the adult).

Using the framework of the myths of Lancelot, with all the adventure, romance, subterfuge and magic, I have tried to investigate his actions, viewed through these three different perspectives.

Following him through his hero's quest, we get to see the human being behind a legend. Maybe this will help us to understand ourselves and those close to us, just a little bit better, and with more generosity and acceptance.

The poem 'The Outlaw' is taken from the poem, 'The Highwayman' by Alfred Noyes, (with apologies.)

Gary Edward Gedall, Lausanne, Switzerland 28 02 2018

gary.gedall@bluewin.ch

Contents

Ch. 0 Epilogue

They are in the courtyard; Lancelot walks his horse towards the gatehouse.

"Why are we not following him?"

"Because our journey is completed, and you have things to ask and to share."

The older Lancelot does not share in this exchange, he follows his younger self with his head and eyes, just until he disappears from view.

"And now he goes to drink himself into oblivion …"

"Until you," the Copper Knight points to Al, "until you come to rescue us."

"Well, I didn't really rescue you."

Now it is Lancelot that responds, "but you did. You really rescued me."

He then turns to his other self. "And, so what is the point of this little adventure?"

In form of a response, he turns back to Al.

"What do you see?"

"What? Here?"

"Yes here."

Al looks lost for a moment, but dutifully looks 'round in all directions. After a while, he chances to look up towards the castle.

There is someone leaning out of the window, she looks like she has been toasting something, goblet still in hand.

"What's she doing there?"

"What do you think, young man?"

He stops to think.

"It was her, she did it, she did it all."

"She? Who? Did what?"

"Can't he see?"

"Lancelot can only be aware of what he saw and noticed when he was really here. I have noticed many more things, but I am unable to communicate these to him."

"So, I can not only see and notice what the other Lancelot saw, but also what you noticed, and I can say what I know?"

"Yes."

"So that is why you brought me with you, so I can tell him what really happened."

"What are you two talking about? It's finished, let us go back, you weary me with your talk."

"Tell, him, tell him everything."

"It was all her."

"All who?"

"Why Morgan, of course."

"Morgan, Morgan le Fey?"

"Yes, yes I believe it was. She must have organised for the Queen to be kidnapped, and for you to catch up to and release her close to Galahaut's castle.

She then disguised herself and gave the drugged wine to Galahaut to give to you, fully knowing that you would both end up in bed together.

You didn't notice, but when you got up the next morning, the bottle had disappeared.

Then she kidnapped Elaine, claiming that she was jealous of her beauty, but when you brought her down from the tower, I was shocked to see that she isn't that beautiful, at all.

Why would she do that, if not to trick you into rescuing her and taking her home to her father?

Then, disguised again, she gives you her special wine, but this time it makes you believe that you are sleeping with Guinevere.

There might even have been something in the drink to help both women beget a child.

But she is still not satisfied, she wants to destroy both you and the queen.

The queen because she would eventually take over the role of keeper of the keys and as Arthur's confident, and you, because you counselled the queen to throw her out.

So she invites you to Camelot, and gets you to write a note to Guinevere, all the time feeding you, once again, the same cursed wine.

She finds a way to get Elaine to come to you, and drugged, you again believe that you are with the queen.

The queen, having been given your note by Morgan, and convinced to go to talk to you, walks in to see you in bed with Elaine.

This is one betrayal too much, and she breaks with you for ever.

The king, he will find out that you have returned to the castle, against his direct orders, will be even more angry against you.

And you, sire… you go quietly and totally mad.”

Ch. 1 Back to the Future

Al turns back to take another look at the elegant witch, but a heavy mist must have blown up from somewhere, it is impossible to see, not even the castle.

So thick and dense, that he dares not even to walk.

"Come," which of the Lancelots has ordered him to advance, is not clear, the voice is also muffled by the swirling fog.

Concerned to be walking blind, he hesitates for moment before accepting the orders of the knight.

Someone grabs onto his arm, just as he is about to fall over an object that has no right to be here.

As they pass through the curtain of smoke, Al finds himself back in the shadowy, dimly lit chamber.

"Careful," it is the 'older' incarnation that is keeping him from tumbling onto the hard, rocky slabs of the cellar floor.

The weird, sweet but musky smell, of the burning weeds, awakens his olfactory memory and returns him to this present moment.

He checks to see just how much the yellow, tallow candles have burnt down since they entered the mirror into the past.

Much to his surprise, they seem to be as big as they were before their fantastic journey began.

He would much like to ask the Copper knight, all sorts of questions, but he is suddenly feeling both famished and totally exhausted, the questions will have to wait.

They leave the dungeon in silence, and return to the same, small dining room where they ate supper, less than a day before.

Al does his best to do justice to the small banquet laid out before them, but he is much too tired to eat more than a bowl of meat stew, before succumbing to the deep exhaustion to has overcome him.

Lancelot succeeds to catch his squire just before his head was about to refill his polished, wooden bowl.

"Methinks that the lad would do well to take a little nap."

"Aye, it has been quite an experience for him, Bruce, help him up to his chamber."

One of the Copper Knight's men appears from
somewhere, and half leads, half carries Al up to his room.

Fully clothed, he drops, both, heavily onto the soft bed
and into a deep, deep sleep.

Ch. 2 Facing the Reality of Now

Al is awoken by the maid fixing the fire. The candles are already burning.

Although much fatigued, his sleep was far from sound. His unconscious insisted in trying to understand and integrate all that he had experienced on the other side of the mystical mirror.

Flashing from time to time, and place to place. It was difficult to keep pace with all that was happening, what was worse, was that, even being a dream, it was hardly any more complicated, disjointed or illogical than what he had just experienced.

Added to that were the many and varied incarnations of Lancelot; all different ages and looks and attitudes and desires.

They would come together, only to begin to argue and then to fight.
Sometimes, some of them would team up against some others, then something would happen, and they would start to disagree amongst themselves.

Bruce, the page, appears at the door, finding Al awake, he informs him that supper is being served, and if he would like to descend, the masters are about to eat.

Al enters to find the two Lancelots in a heated discussion.

"That is not me, that is not who I am?"

"It is who you were, and maybe, you've not changed that much, since."

"I was younger then, thou art unjust to take us back there."

They notice Al.

"Come," his host waves him into the room. "Come sit."

He enters a little hesitantly, wary of the row that he is surely about to be embroiled in.

He takes the open seat, there is a momentary silence. Looking at the twin knights, he has a most weird thought. 'They want me to be the judge of something,'

The lowly, orphan, innkeeper's lackey, is about to be supplicated by his own master, and his double, and to arbitrate between the two of them. Not that he would use those specific terms, but they were pretty much the thoughts that passed through his head.

His master turns towards him.

"Al, this has not been a true and fair representation of who I am."

"But I don't understand," already he is lost and scared to upset either one of them,

"I was told that these were your own memories."

"Well, yes they were, sort of," he is trying to explain something that is not obvious, maybe not even to himself. "Yes, they showed what I remember of what happened, but that wasn't really who I was, or how it passed."

Al, looks helplessly towards the Copper Knight.

"We have debated the whole afternoon on this one question. This is our past, he just cannot abide that we see it as such."

"I am not that man."

"Why not?" Al does not stutter, he is cross examining one of the most famous knights ever, calmly and logically.

"Because that man, even if I was once him, has betrayed his oath of loyalty and honour."

"But you did, we did. It is our truth, we carry that guilt. Do not add cowardice to our heavy burden of sins."

"Why did you take me with you?" He now turns to question the other knight.

"As I have said, we needed a witness, we needed someone that could see beyond 'his' own vision."

"But you, you were tricked. She tricked you. She got you to drink that wine, the cursed wine. You were under a spell." Al tries to help out his proud sponsor.

"Yes, I was under a spell, a spell of lust. I lusted after the queen, whether or not the wine was drugged, 'tis of no matter, I had already sinned in my heart."

"So you admit it? You were weak, and you gave yourself to your base desire?"

"Your game is to prove that I am without honour? Fine, échec et mat, you win." He gets up brusquely, "come, let's be going".

Al looks sadly at the food, then at the Copper Knight.

"Running away, once again?"

"We have nothing more to do here. You've well shown me my lacks and weaknesses, I think that I've seen and heard all that you would wish to share with me."

"No, Lancelot, sorry, but you've understood nothing, but maybe it is still too soon."

"Yes, it must surely be that, but do not worry yourself, I will be back."

"When you are ready to hear and see?"

"No, when I am ready to best you, and take back what is rightfully mine."

And with that he strides out, only stopping himself from slamming the heavy, wood as he notices the young man, sheepishly rushing out to keep up with him.

The last image that Al has of the other Lancelot, is that of an older man, sadly shaking his head…

Ch. 3 Back to Safety

Lancelot would have done better to wait inside while the horses were being prepared.

It is getting rather cold, but he must have been much too angry to stay still. So he just paces, there and back, in the dark, courtyard, until he can finally leave.

It was Bruce that brought Al's horse to him. He was surprised and pleased to find that there was a heavy, riding cloak thrown over the saddle.

Bruce helps him to throw it on.

"It'll be a long, cold ride."

"Thank you."

"And if you'd be a little hungry." He passes him a grey, cloth sack. "God speed."

"Goodbye, Bruce, and thank you." Touched by the kindness of the young page, and maybe others, behind the scenes, Al kicks the horse into motion and follows his master into the long, dark night.

Somewhere, not so far off, an owl hoots, it's sharp yellow eyes blink, that is to be all that they will hear for quite some hours.

They travel in silence, Al digs often into his sack of surprise delights; where he finds, fresh rolls, chicken drumsticks and pork ribs.

As he has slept, however badly, all through the afternoon, he is not tired.

Warmed by his new, heavy, woollen cloak, and nourished by the generosity of his guardian angels of the keep, he is feeling, not so surprisingly, quite good.

They must have ridden for at least three or four hours before, finally, Lancelot gives in to his need for sleep, and knocks-up a sleepy tavern owner, to find them beds for the rest of the short night.

For next three days, they do nothing but eat, sleep and ride.

As Lancelot doesn't seem to be open to talking, not even to share their final destination, Al chooses discretion, and contents himself to enjoy the riding and the open road.

It is nearly evening when they pass a massive sandstone complex.

"Furness Abbey," Lancelot turns and the ice melts, "one of the richest and most influential abbeys in all of Christendom."

"Where are we going?" He couldn't miss this unique opportunity of communication, to not inquire of their destination.

"Why to Sorelais, of course. If there is one human being in this world that I can count on to support me, it would be my great friend, Galahaut."

Al digs back into the shared memories of the knight's past and conjures up the face of the king of this local island.

They stop at a rich looking inn with the image of a great wooden tower swinging on the painted sign.

"What's that?"

"Oh, before they built Piel Castle, there was a lookout tower."

"But I seem to remember that Peel Castle was on the island."

"They are both on islands, one is just over there, the other we will get to on the morrow, they are written differently." He doesn't explain any more, maybe he doesn't actually know how to write the name of either.

The next morning, they cross over to the island of Piel on a flat barge, before boarding the boat for Sorelais.

The early morning air is fresh and stimulating, it whips the waves into a frenzy of frosty peaks.

The seagulls dip and dive into swelling seas, hoping to find a tasty titbit or two.

Their claw-like, yellow beaks, snapping at the hidden treasures below.

Some circle, benefitting from the wind's powerful uplift.

While the others, perch, watching and waiting, with piercing, yellow eyes.

Al, having nothing better to do, throws bits of the old bread from his sack, to the greedy gulls.

As he knows no-one on the boat, other than Lancelot, who is again in a pensive, uncommunicative mood, after finishing feeding the flock, he finds himself a quiet corner, rolls himself in his new cloak, and doses off.

The hours pass in weird mixture of falling into and out of sleep, dreaming or remembering the experience of this passage from Lancelot's memories.

"Doth thou plan to stay aboard, or come to meet our hosts?" His master gives him a gentle kick on the butt.

"W'w'what?" The shock re-awakens his stutter.

"We are arrived."

Al shakes himself awake, almost falls over his cloak as he all but jumps to his feet.

"Careful, there's no fire," the knight smiles as he turns to check on their horses, that are being readied to disembark.

He gathers up his few belongings and heads towards the heavy ramp. The horizontal slats ensure that he doesn't slip down the slippery, wet wood.

There is a small crowd waiting to greet them, surely Lancelot would not have come unannounced, just that he had not been aware of his master having sent or received any communications.

There were surely many instances when they had been separated when, he would have had ample opportunity to ask for and have been given the invitation for this visit.

He is now in the arms of a great bear of a man. Al is shocked to realise that this is the same Galahaut from Lancelot's memories.

Only this man is much, much older. Heavier, and with both hair and beard, richly peppered with shiny strands of grey hair.

During the experience through the mirror, he had never thought to question exactly when the events had occurred.

Now he realises that the young girl that they encountered on their very first connection with Lancelot's memories, five or six, to his reckoning, can be no other than the Lady Angelique.

A mature woman, even quite old to be as yet unmarried, she must be already, well past her twenty years, closer to twenty-five if local gossip is to be believed.

Which means that the young prince, tall and gangly, with wild red hair, now being presented to the noble guest, must be Erik, now surely passed his eighteenth summer.

Being totally ignored is something that stable boys, tavern workers and servants are quite used to.

So when the others mount up and lead off, without so much as a glance in his direction, he simply takes his horse, and follows.

Ch. 4 Sanctuary

Al finds himself particularly bored, his current responsibilities towards his knight limit themselves to attending the afternoon and evening meals and serving his master his wine.

A stupid and pointless task, as there are more than enough other servants to do this specific task.

Only,

Dena.

Dena is Erik's younger sister. She is some years younger than Al, a beautiful young lady with flaming hair and raven eyes.

He is totally captivated by her, her every move, every look, every word.

However, he is not in love with her.

She is a paradox for him.

He has had his fair share of sexual fantasies, and, although still a virgin, has not stayed that way for want of desire.

She fascinates him, yes, but excites him, no.

Not so surprisingly, his intense interest does not go unnoticed.

"Squire, what doth thou?"

He looks up from his endeavours and, stupidly, points his sticky rag towards the leather object.

"I, I, w'was p'p'polishing the, the saddle." He was not prepared for her to appear at this moment. His verbal tick proving just how shocked he is.

Appearing to totally ignore his speech impediment, she continues in a comfortable, and relaxed fashion.

"I've noticed you staring at me, when I am at table. Last night you almost poured the wine over your knight."

He goes to say something to contradict her, although nothing succeeds to exit his mouth.

"And yet, I feel that you neither wish to possess nor be possessed by me, I am very sensitive to this."

"Y' you are v'v'very sensitive, ma'am."

"Yes, yes, I am."

"I hear that you are to thank for having helped Lancelot to regain his health."

"I, I, d'did little."

"No matter, he speaks very highly of you."

"H' he does?"

She smiles at him.

"You are like no one that I have ever met, and yet, methinks that I already know you."

Such a strange, impossible idea to have, and yet, it also tugs a cord within the young man's soul.

"I, I t'too."

Unceremoniously she drags a mounting box over to his corner of the saddlery

She then seats herself down, facing the uncomfortable young man.

He is feeling hot and flushed, she is scanning him, intensely.

It is,
   almost as if,
      she just might,
         through some visual clue,
            uncover that hidden, secret,
………   of their most particular connection.

He breaks the link and turns away from her, busying himself with polishing the saddle.

"Which is your horse?"

Without turning or thinking, he points out towards stables where his small steed is quietly waiting in its narrow box.

"You know, not all squires have their own horse."

"It's not mine, my master has given me use of it." When not conversing directly with her, it is easier to master his speech.

"Not all squires have the sole use of one of their master's horses." She was being intentionally pedantic.

"Yes, not all squires have the sole use of one of their master's horses." Not really understanding why, he turns and smiles at her.

"Will you take me for a ride? Erik is always too busy now, and no one else rides fast enough to make it fun."

And so it came to pass that that very next afternoon, after clearly checking that it was acceptable for everyone, Al took the Lady Dena riding.

Not to say that he didn't have to pass through two rather unpleasant interviews, one with Lancelot, the other with Erik.

"The Lady Dena will be in your charge, and you will be honour-bound to see that no harm comes to her."

"I will die before I let anyone come near to the Lady."

Lancelot stops for a moment before continuing.

"I lost my honour by not containing my own lust."

"Sire?"

"She is nearly fifteen, she is a young woman."

Al is quite lost, he is having difficulty joining the pieces of the conversation together.

"You will not ravish her."

"What? But no!" The proverbial penny has dropped.

"Sire, I accord that she is a handsome woman, but I have not those type of feelings for her. It seems that we both feel as brother and sister."

"And it had better stay that way." And the knight, playfully whacks him on the shoulder.

The interview with the young lord was similar although rather more formal.

"If thou lest any evil befall my sister, you will know a suffering that will make death but a release."

On the other hand, she showed no signs of concern, and after that first, short, afternoon ride, everyone cooled down and no more was ever suggested about his intentions towards his new ward.

Ch. 5 Kidnapped

In truth, it could be possible to gallop the whole of the length of the island in about an hour, but they rarely went much more than a few miles in any direction.

There were forests to walk through and fields to gallop round, that was enough to get them out and give the horses a pleasant exercise.

She would like to gallop at full tilt for ten or fifteen minutes, but that was all that she seemed to need to get the adrenalin rush that she craved.

Only, today, she fancied to go a little further and investigate parts of her little island that she didn't yet know.

They had been trotting for about an hour, following the steep coastline in a counter-clockwise direction, when she asked to stop and partake of a little picnic that she had asked to be prepared.

And so they found a small copse of trees, released the horses to graze and sat down, backs resting on the solid beeches, to partake in honey cakes and light ale.

How relaxing, lounging in the sun, stomachs full of sweet flavours, listening to song of a lone bird, somewhere far off, yet, from the sound, coming ever closer.

How long they had been followed, counting in hours or in days, they could have no idea, but within moments of their descending from the horses, out from behind the small wood, they came.

Al has no time to react. A coarse, woollen sack is thrown over his head and pulled down to block his arms. He is then roughly pushed forward.

As he is already sitting down, it is not to make him fall, but to give them the space to tie something round his body, rendering him incapable to move his arms at all.

"Right, get them up," he can still hear the orders of one of the assailants. Not surprisingly, it is a man's voice.

"Careful with the bellibone, she's worth her weight in gold, she ain't to be 'armed."

"This one, we could just throw 'im off of the edge, and be done with 'im."

"No killin', I said that I'm in if there's no killin'."

"Grig."

"I'm no coward, it's just that killin' for no good reason is a sin."

"And this is a straight-fingered job?"

"Maybe it's a crime, but it's no a sin."

"Will you two jus' get 'em down to the sea and into the boat, anyone could come and see us."

"Yeh, get movin' priest."

"And some day you'll rot in Hell."

"Tamp down, both of you."

Al is heaved onto someone's shoulders, while another takes his feet. There is no point in struggling, he has no way to get out of the sack.

And even if he could, there were at least three men that he would have to deal with before he could even escape, never mind the possibility of rescuing Dena.

The descent to the beach wasn't totally without incident and he was almost dropped several times.

One of the problems was that the guy holding his legs must be taller than the one carrying him, so his legs being behind, and higher up the slope put extra weight on the other.

Finally they changed the order, and his feet preceded him, and he was kept, pretty much horizontal.

The boat trip began, if anything in an awfully boring way, that is, until he realised that he had an unfortunately strong urge to relieve himself.

"I need to pee."

"You can't be serious."

"Just hold it." The short guy, (the one that had carried him on his shoulder), was really a pain.

"Look I need to pee, things are bad enough without me peeing on myself."

"Sorry, but it's just not possible." That one must be the boss.

"I could help him." If this guy is so nice, what's he doing with this gang of crooks?

"You want to do that?"

"Please, I really need to go."

"Okay, you can help him if y' want to. What about you missy?"

"I think that I will manage for the moment, but please promise me one thing."

"What?"

"Just keep the sack over my head until he's finished."

There is a silence that follows. Al assumes that the crooks are, if anything impressed that, even in this situation, she can find something humorous to respond.

In any other circumstance he would be mortified with shame to allow another man to help him in this way, but the need is so great, all he can feel is a deep appreciation for the guy.

"Thank you. I know that you didn't need to do that."

"Well, he's a trundle-tail:saint, ain't ya'?"

"That's enough Michael, let it go." And that was that until they finally got to shore.

They must have been plotting this for a while, for once they arrived on the other shore, it took hardly any time before a cart rattled up to them, and they were bundled in.

They were relieved to notice that there must be piles of old sacks covering the hard wood of the floor of the transport.

Time, when there is little to judge it by, can seem relatively short, or interminably long.

Here, shaken up and down by the fixed wooden wheels on the uneven surfaces that they were rolling over, time might have slowed down to a crawl, as they seemed to travel on, for-ever.

Eventually, they stop and they are helped down to the ground. From there, they are directed into some sort of building, and up several flights of stairs.

Many, many stairs.

They enter a room and he feels the ropes being loosened.

"You get yourselves out of the sacks," the leader informs them before they hear the door close and lock.

After some jumping and wriggling he manages to loosen them enough for them to drop to the floor and is wondering how to remove the sack, when someone comes to his rescue.

Dena has already released herself and helps pull the rough material up and over his head.

Instinctively, she falls into his arms, and he holds the young, fragile flower, in his safe, protective grip.

It seems so normal, and so right.

Ch. 6 Imprisoned

The room is quite large, although it is not easy to see as there is no light and it was already evening.

The floor is made out of rough wood, there are two mattresses with woollen blankets left against one of the rough-stone walls, the windows are no more than thin slits to let in air and light, the roof is quite high and the rafters that support it are long, heavy and inhabited.

The black, hanging shapes have been disturbed by their entrance, several pairs of beady, yellow eyes had magically appeared. Only now, noticing that these, great, two legged creatures are none flying specimens, the mini orbs are blinking out, two at a time.

Dena shudders a little and digs deeper into Al's safe body.

"Look, what's that?" He has noticed something. In the corner of the room, furthest from the locked door in which they must have entered, there seems to be another, though small door.

He uncurls himself from her, gets up, and goes to investigate.

To their great surprise and relief, the door opens onto a very tiny, but particularly appreciated little room, A room with one seat, that has a hole under it. – A toilet.

Dena sighs a massive sigh, and rushes to relieve herself.

Al goes and sits on one of the beds, lost and confused about all that has happened to them

'What do they want with Dena? They must want to bargain her for something. Maybe they will try to ransom her.

Yes, her father would gladly pay a tidy sum to get her back, that's why they said to not harm her.

Yeh, she'll be okay.' It is then that another, more sobering thought strikes him.

'But who would be willing to pay anything for me? They said that they thought to kill me, to throw me off a cliff. I have no value, no-one will part with good silver for a simple squire.

Lancelot's a good man, but I have no real value to him, no, I suppose that they're just keeping me to keep her company.'

And so she finds him in a rather desperate state.

"I'm sure that it will be fine. They haven't hurt us, they've even been quite gentle with you."

Al stops for a second, debating whether to share his dark reflections with her, only to decide that it would only make her concerned for him, and that would, in turn, make matters worse for her.

"I couldn't do anything, they were too fast. I wish that I could have had more chance to defend you," he lies.

"They were much too quick. They must have planned this for a while, and had been waiting in hiding for their opportunity.

If anything, it was my fault. If I hadn't wanted to explore the island a bit more, and had stayed where we were safe, we wouldn't be in this mess.

It's for me to apologise to you."

"If they'd been waiting like that, they'd have got us sooner or later," Al wants to let her off the hook, there is no point in her feeling guilty.

She is back in his arms, he is, at the same time happy to have this intimate contact with her, and yet, every so slightly concerned about his lack of any sexual desire towards her.

'Maybe it's because I'm just a humble, orphan squire, and she's a princess, and 'cus it's just not possible, that it just doesn't feel possible.'

Of course this is not at all true. For you see, the young princess that he saw in Lancelot's vision, when he first came into Camelot. The girl that he more than just glanced at, was no other than the Lady Angelique.

The very same Lady Angelique who would, on occasion trot past the tavern where

he lived with his adoptive family, and who he was, ever so secretly, in love with.

This choice piece of information and powerful counter-argument, he succeeded painlessly, to keep from himself.

Satisfied with his own inner reflection, exhausted, he fell into a light doze. Presumably, so did Dena.

If left alone, they likely would have quickly fallen into a quite deep sleep, if not for the heavy lock in the door, which is being turned, so as to allow the door to be opened.

The tall guy enters, while his short partner stands guard on the threshold.

He is carrying to steaming bowls.

"He's some grub, it's not much, but it hot and good." Al is surprised to realise that he is actually apologising, but before he succeeds to find anything appropriate to respond, his companion has already started to speak.

"That is very kind of you, we thank you."

The guy smiles, "we don't mean you any harm miss, we just get a job to do."

"And that job is to kidnap me?"

" 'Fraid so."

"Shut y' trap, you's too talkative," his associate reminds him of his role.

"Nihtslæp," he smiles and leaves.

The bowls contain a vegetable soup and some chunks of rough bread. As was often the custom, there are no spoons.

They first drink the hot, tasty liquid, then they use the pieces of bread to catch the bits of veg and use them to carry them to their mouths. Finally using the last morsels to mop up the final remains.

They hadn't uttered a single syllable from the moment that began eating, until the final drops were absorbed into the bread and deposited into their willing mouths.

"I have eaten many a feast, that I have not relished as much as this," she is relaxed and smiling.

"I think that we will be safe and well looked after, our worst danger is likely to be boredom," is she laughing at him.

"I hope that I am not boring, m'lady."

"Al, you are the sweetest boy that I've ever met. No, you are not boring, I was jesting. I'm sure that you have many tales to tell of your master's brave exploits.

And," she catches herself, "and your part in these stories of bravery and heroics."

"Although I know well many of the legends of Sir Lancelot, I have only been his squire for the shortest of time. I am really only a simple inn helper, that has had the great, good fortune to have somehow pleased the great knight. That is all."

"Well, you are now my hero, and that is good enough for me."

She stops and looks around for a moment.

"I would prefer this cot," she points to one of the beds, "if that is acceptable to you."

Al is not used to noble ladies asking him if something suits him or not.

"M'lady, please choose as, as, as you wish." That awful stammer is threatening to return.

"Then, I will choose this one. Good night noble squire."

"Good night, m'lady."

As she is now some feet away, he cannot see clearly in the semi darkness, but he fancies that she smiles in his direction.

"Good night Al."
He doesn't dare to call her by her first name.

"G' night." And they settle down for the night.

Ch. 7 Released

They are awakened by the door being unlocked and opened.

Their friendly jailer has brought them bread, cheese and two mugs of light ale.

Not waiting for a thank you, and still under the serious, watchful eye of his fellow criminal, he quickly turns and leaves.

The two, young prisons, vaguely shrug their shoulders and attack the food.

Well, Al starts to pounce on to it, until he realises and remembers exactly who his cell mate is.

"M'lady, after you," he makes an effort at an elegant gesture.

"Come, we can eat together," but he hesitates at taking either the loaf of bread or block of cheese to break them in his grubby hands.

"Here, let me serve you," she, noticing his hesitation.

She breaks him off a large chunk of bread and healthy portion of cheese, before helping herself to some smaller servings.

"Thank you," he mumbles, and begins to eat.

They had hardly finished when the door opens again.

This must be the chief, they hadn't yet seen his face.

He is carrying a scroll of parchment.

"Get up, boy." Al goes towards the man. He is of about the same height, medium build, with scruffy dark hair and black, raven eyes.

You are to return t' the island and give this to Lord Galahaut. You are not to open it, 'tis for his eyes only. If you fail this, she will die."

He gives him the scroll and ushers him out of the tower.

"God's speed," was all that he can capture before being pushed towards the stairs.

The early morning sunlight hits him full in the face, and he is momentarily blinded.

He would likely have fallen heavily onto the hard earth, if the kidnapper had not reacted and grabbed his arm.

"Careful!".

"Thanks."

"Get up onto the cart. You'll be taken back to Barro' island. Here's crossing money." He gives Al some coins, more than enough to pay for the boat trip.

Al looks around a bit stupidly.

"What cart?"

Now it is the turn of the kidnapper to look lost.

"Michael! Michael! Where in the devil's name are you?"

The little, nasty one appears from behind a building.

"Where's the cart?" Michael is on foot, and a little out of breath.

"Idyot's gone and took the horses f' another job."

"When will they be back?"

"D'no, before lunch, so the ostler told me." He then looks towards Al, "What y goin' to do with 'im?"

"You can take him back up to the tower."

"Why me?"

"Well I've just been up and down, it's your turn."

"You can go sard yourself, I've been runnin' all morning." He takes a shifty look 'round. "What if we just left 'im in here?" He points towards a door in the building.

"What would Faron say."

"A curse on 'im, he's fine for telling us what to do, but we's the one's doin' it. I'm not takin' them's stairs right now."

"Fine, You go and wait in here. And don't you go running off."

Before Al could even think to respond, Michael thought to add.

"If you don't deliver that letter, and Galahaut don't agree before tomorro' night, Faron says that he'll sell her to the gypsies."

Al has heard tales about this dangerous, wandering tribe, and is suitably impressed with the threat.

He is bundled into the tiny store room.

"And don't you go reading that letter!"

"Don't be daft," Michael interjects, " 'e can't read. We can't read, why d'y think 'e can read?"

"Well, just saying so. And I can read, just not so fast."

And, arguing, they leave him to his own devices.

Ch. 8 The Letter

Maybe it's something that most of us first experience during the 'terrible two's ', but when we are specifically instructed what we are not allowed to do, the general reaction that many of us have, - is to want to do it.

Al had obviously wondered what was written on the scroll that he had been given, but had been too scared of the consequences to think to open it.

Here, now, left to his own devices, with nothing better to do, the temptation is just too strong.

He pulls out the rolled parchment and turns it over in his hands.

'I know that I shouldn't, but they've kidnapped Dena, and I need to know why."

Of cause the logic is flawed, but we all have a great capacity to deceive ourselves, when we desire to.

'I'll just say that the seal got broken, that I fell down, that I fell on it'.

And to try and make it look like that, he crushes the object against a table, with the flat of his hand.

By the usual laws of the universe, it doesn't work. It finally takes him four tries before he succeeds to crack open the hard, wax shield.

Sire,

Thou hast chosen to deny my envoys access to your noble person.

You have refused all attempts on my part to communicate with you.

Thus, you have left me no choice but to force you to negotiate by threat.

By grace of my trusted contacts in your kingdoms, I have heard of a plot that you have to invade and oust King Arthur from his realm.

That, even now, you are amassing a secret army, and that, before the month's end, you plan to effect this. For the moment, my attention is elsewhere, and my desire for Arthur's throne is not my priority.

However, I could, if the whim would come to me, crush your aspirations, and inform my cousin of your plans.

But, that would bring me no gain.

Galahaut, I am prepared to offer you a pact.

I will keep my own council as to your plans from Arthur, return your daughter, unharmed in any way, and you, you will capture the queen, Guinevere and bring her, likewise, unharmed, to me.

Give me your oath as a knight and a king, and your daughter will be safe, once again in your keep.

Of this, I give you my word.

In God we trust

Mordred.

He rereads it twice, having great effort to accept to written words, fixed on the creamy, stained paper.

Then, in a semi daze, lets it drop. Strong emotions and negative news can bring on a feeling of heavy exhaustion.

He just needs to run away, into sleep. There is no other appropriate action that occurs to him.

But first, he needs to roll back up the letter and put it back in his jerkin pocket.

The action is quite mechanical, and once done, he slouches down in a dusty corner, as if trying to hide himself from the cruel reality, of which, he has just become privy.

'She's just a pawn in a sick game of power and greed.' The thought brings an increasing feeling of irritation and anger.

Ignoring the fact that he is interfering in the power games of two powerful kings, he decides to try and take matters into his own hands.

The window is nothing more than a hole in the wall covered with some old cloth.

He pulls across the faded material, and pokes his head out, there are some people passing, but he sees neither of the two kidnappers.

He hadn't heard them locking the door, and, testing it, he proves to be right, it opens without problem.

He door to the tower is not locked either, and in almost no time at all, he is before the heavy door of their prison.

The key is in the lock.

"What?" She is more than a little shocked to see him enter.

"No time, come we must get out now."

As there is nothing to take, other than to throw on her riding cloak, they are quickly descending the staircase.

Without thinking, he has taken her hand, and is gently dragging her down the stairs.

He has already experienced the shock of entering into the full sunlight, after the gloom of the tower. She, being pulled forward, also stumbles into the street.

He catches her around the waist, a balletic movement.

"Where now?"

He has no idea, he hadn't even thought beyond getting her out of the locked room.

Doubt and fear wash over him like an icy wave.

'What now? Yes, where to go?'

His hesitation gives her the answer, he might be lost, but she is a princess, self-assurance is part of her education.

"We need to get away from here. Come."

Now it is her, dragging him.

"What is it?" He has stopped in front of a torn poster.

"The Faron Show, International Acrobats."

"Is it so necessary to exhibit to me, at this moment, that you can read?"

"Look, it's them." There is worn drawing of three people's heads. One is Michael, the other is the tall kidnapper, and the third, with small beady, bird eyes could well be the third.

"Acrobats? Truth, they didn't really seem very professional."

"And you know how professional kidnappers are supposed to behave?"

"Professional or not, we would'st be best to try not to encounter them again."

From around the next corner they could hear raised voices. They advance cautiously only to discover Michael arguing with a young man leading two horses.

"Look, I's got to get to Barra' and back. So's I needs them now, okay?"

"Them's not your horses, you only pays when you needs 'em."

"And we needs 'em now, you put the 'ole consarn in danger."

The stable-boy hands the horses over to Michael.

"Ju' see that Faron don't forget to pay for 'em." The short criminal makes a rude gesture with his thumb and front teeth, before taking the beasts.

"I've got an idea." Now it is the turn of the squire to take the lead.

They surreptitiously follow the man and the horses to a little court yard. In which, presumably, the same cart in which they were bought here, waits.

Michael starts to busy himself hitching up the horses.

"I'll go and distract him, you climb into the cart and hide yourself under the sacks."

He releases her hand and boldly walks over to the front of the cart.

"What you doin' 'ere? You wus told to wait for me."

"Got bored, you were taking so long. So I thought I would go out for a walk, and then I saw you with the horses, well here I am."

He has intentionally placed himself facing the horses, that way, Michael, to talk to him, has to turn with his back to the cart.

Al, can clearly see that Dena, has succeeded to climb into the cart, and has disappeared from view.

"I would also like to get back as soon as possible, that way I can deliver my message and never have to see you again."

"If you never sees me again, then 'er Ladyship gets sold to the gypsies. You has to come back wiv a note from the King."

"What sort of note."

"Ow in Bard's name am I supposed to know? Jus' that he agrees wiv' that what's in the letter you is carryin'. Come, let's be off."

He has finished hitching up the horses and is leading them out of the constricted opening of the yard, before jumping onto the rail.

"Get up and let's go."

Ch. 9 The Return

The return was much more comfortable for Al, although he was a little concerned for the princess.

Their driver was clearly in a pretty foul mood, and was only intent in getting back to town to do, what-ever he was intent on doing. Hence, he was driving like a maniac!

From time to time, he heard, or imagined that he heard a faint cry after a particularly violent lurch of the cart.

Truly the return trip seemed much, much shorter than that of the night before.

For one thing, they had quite quickly joined the same road that he had rode with Lancelot, so he knew where they were and could already estimate, roughly how long it would take.

And for the other, he was trying to decide what to say and do when they finally got back to Sorelais.

The simplest thing would be just to deliver the letter and leave it to Galahaut to decide what to do with it.

Fine, but what about Galahaut's plans to invade Camelot, must he tell Lancelot, or not?

Would his knight join with his friend and avenge himself against the king that had had him exiled?

Or would he break with Galahaut and rush to defend his love, the queen?

And then, what of Dena, would she know of her father's plans? More than likely not. So, should he be the one to tell her that she was just a pawn in some complicated plot to invade a kingdom and dispose of the deposed queen?

In the end, the simplest thing would be to give the letter to Galahaut, but to also share its contents with Lancelot.

It is not for a simple squire to take decisions for his betters.

That decided, he relaxes and tries to enjoy the ride, hoping that the princess will not hate him forever for suggesting that she hid in the back of the cart.

They arrive at the short ferry to Barra island and Al jumps down from his seat.

Michael makes to leave immediately, Al, thinking fast, rushes up to the head of the horses.

"What y' doin'? Y're blocking the horses."

"Just want to say goodbye to the horses. You never know when I might meet them again. Horses remember people."

"Jes' get out o' way, or your horses will remember that you're the idiyot that they done run down."

Hoping that she has had the time to got off, he jumps out of the way as the driver roughly shakes the reins and starts the horses off at a fast trot.

From out of nowhere, Al receives a nasty punch in the kidneys.

"Ouch!"

"Next time you hide in the back of a cart from Hades."

"I'm sorry, I didn't think that he'd drive like that."

"It's fine," she smiles at him, "it got us both here, it was a good plan."

Al is most relieved that she isn't going to hate him forever over his scheme.

Unfortunately, one bad thought is replaced by another.

"Oh, no, I fear that I do not have enough to pay for the passage for both of us. He was quite generous with what he gave me, but it might not be enough."

"Aren't you forgetting something?"

Al looks suitably confused.

"I am the princess of that little island over there. Finding passage will pose no difficulty. Come squire, your lady is ready to return to her castle."

She is laughing at him, but in a most friendly fashion. Al gives an exaggerated bow and followers her to the boats.

Ch. 10 Revelations

The boat ride back to Sorelais was stressful for Al, he was worried that she would ask him if he had any idea why she was taken.

If she did, how would he react? Would he tell her the truth? He'd already planned to tell her nothing. And yet, was he capable to tell her a cold lie? To lie directly to her face?

Fortunately, the conversation never happened.

The tossing that she endured in the back of the cart had totally exhausted her, and with the gentle rocking of the boat, it took her no time to fall back asleep.
She might have been comfortable to sleep on his shoulder, but he was much less so.

Clearly there were people, here on the boat, who knew who she is, but not necessarily who he was.

If the king found out that his only female offspring was openly sleeping on the shoulder of a humble squire, what might his reaction be?

Not having any other option, he smiles and shrugs his shoulders if he notices anyone looking at them.

She finally rouses herself, gives him a sleepy smile, stretches, gets up, and goes for a walk.

Her total indifference to the situation that she has put him in irritates him, but only for a moment.

As, after all, if she doesn't think anything about draping herself over someone that is nothing more than a servant, and in broad daylight, then what should he worry?

It only takes a few minutes after the boat has docked before the two find themselves on a carriage, on their way back to the castle.

Someone must have ridden ahead to inform the household, for there was quite a reception committee waiting for them when they arrived.

As would be expected, all the attention was directed towards Dena, and she was quickly herded off by her family and courtiers.

Al slowly climbs down from the fancy cart.

"Methinks that there must be quite a story to be told."

He spins 'round to discover his master, casually leaning against a post.

He must have arrived with the crowd, only to separate himself and wait, holding up the wall, situated, directly behind Al's seat.

"Sire, you startled me."

The knight beams a huge smile, "I thought that I might have lost my loyal squire.

You had us worried for a while."

"We were kidnapped."

"Why?" The obvious question, now to choose how to respond.

"Would it be acceptable for us to walk a little?"

He wasn't sure if the knight would understand his request?

"A stroll is always a good idea, especially if you haven't had the opportunity to move in hours." Maybe he did understand the subtle request.

They walk for a good fifteen minutes before Lancelot stops them. There are a few sparse trees. Not enough to hide anyone behind, but big enough to lean on.

He makes himself comfortable before signalling his squire to do the same.

"It seems that a certain discretion is the order of the day."

"There are things that maybe you should know, that it is best, no one else knows that you do."

"Since when have you begun to talk in riddles?" Lancelot is still showing signs of being in a good mood. If anything, he is as amused, as he is intrigued.

"We were kidnapped under orders from Mordred."

"Mordred, what would he want with Dena?" It is clear that no one would even, for one second think that he, a nobody, would have any value.

"He wanted to force Galahaut to offer him …," he takes a gulp, no knows that Lancelot's good humour is about to melt away. " … the Lady Guinevere."

"And just how does he think that my friend is going to be able to that?" He still seems more intrigued than angry, that's good.

"He believes that Galahaut is planned to invade Camelot."

"But that's just nonsense." He shakes his head, as if that will convince Al.

"Maybe it is, but that is why we were kidnapped. He promised to release Lady Dena only if he agreed to give him the queen, otherwise, he'd sell her to the gypsies."

"There are no gypsies in England, at least, not to my knowledge."

"Well that's what they told me."

"Who told you?"

"The kidnappers."

"And they told you about Mordred and his desire for Lady Guinevere and about Galahaut's plan to invade Camelot?"

"No, I read that in the letter that I am supposed to give to the king."

"And they let you read it?"

"Of course not, they don't even know that I can."

Suddenly, a smallish bird with a grey head and orangey-cream underparts streaked in black, swoops down between them.

"What's that?" Al jumps back in surprise.

"Just a Merlin, nothing to be afraid of." Then getting up.

"Come, I must be heading back. If there's any truth in this story, then I need to confront Galahaut with it."

And so it is that they set their faces to the direction of the castle.

Only, they are intercepted even before they get there.

Ch. 11 Two Messages.

Waiting for them is a young man, someone not unknown to Al.

"Jay?"

Jay, Al's adoptive parent's son, was now dressed in the attire of a page of the court of King Arthur.

"Sire, Al," always the most correct possible. He hands the knight a scroll, and waits politely while it is being read.

Al, noticing the strong reaction on his master's face, dares to ask.

"What is it? What has happened?" Jay looks totally scandalised by his adoptive brother's inappropriateness.

However, Lancelot reacts, unexpectedly by responding.

"It is from their Majesties, they have heard of both the kidnapping and of the letter.
We are to say nothing to anyone of our knowledge and are to meet with my cousin Sir Lionel, who will arrive tomorrow."

He turns to the younger brother.

"Jay, you will stay in the tavern, here," he dips his hand in his pocket. The leather pouch sways as he pulls some coins out of it.

"Thank you most kindly, sire. And may I ask just something else?"

"Yes?"

"The members of the court know me Alexander, I would most appreciate it if you might refer to me by that name."

"Fine, Alexander, have a pleasant night."

He then turns to Al.

"You know nothing of the kidnapper's reasons for taking the Lady Dena, and it was just by happenstance that you managed to escape."

"But, that is exactly the truth."

Lancelot smiles, "good boy," and he playfully slaps him on the shoulders.

"You must be hungry, go and rustle yourself something nice from the kitchen. If anyone should ask any questions, it is the Knight, Sir Lancelot that commands."

And so they enter into the waiting castle.

Ch. 12 An Offer That Cannot be Refused

Sir Lionel is waiting for them in a secluded nook of the smoky tavern. Jay was sitting with him, but as he saw the two arrive, he respectfully slid away.

Again he is surprised to see that Al is expected to stay and participate in the discussion.

He has dark curly hair, a thin face and a droopy moustache, he is wearing nondescript riding clothes. Huddled in his corner, he is clearly not looking for attention.

"Cousin," he raises slightly, and salutes Lancelot. He maybe acknowledges Al with a tilt of the head. He must have expected the squire's presence, as he now, simply ignores that he is there.

"We have heard of the letter and the secret amassing of an army, with which to attack Camelot."

"I have neither seen nor heard of any whisper of this army, nor this attack." Lancelot is not ready to believe that his best friend is preparing to attack the King.

"The kidnap and the letter should be proof enough. However, the King confirms that he has spies that can confirm this. It is how he has gotten to know about the kidnapping and the letter."

They cease talking as a serving girl appears with tankards.

Lancelot plays with the heavy, metal mug.

Long moments pass.

"So, what is it that their Majesties wish of me?" He asks, eventually.

"Arthur fears that Galahaut has magicians and druids in his pay that will use magic to gain an advantage over him."

"But Arthur has Merlin."

"Yes, but Galahaut has the Uffington sceptre, made by Merlin himself, it is capable to block any sort of magical attack."

"Hmmm." Lancelot is thinking.

"As long as Galahaut has the sceptre, he has a dangerous advantage over Camelot."

"And I am supposed to steal it?"

"There is no other way."

He suddenly remembers. "But I have been banished by the King and the Queen has sworn never to speak to me again."

"Much has happened in the short while that you have been absent. Merlin has discovered that Arthur's sister, Morgan has been interfering in matters that she should, better not have."

"Which means?" Lancelot is suddenly much more attentive.

"That your errors might be forgiven, if you were to succeed to save Camelot by retrieving the Uffington sceptre."

"So, I regain the good graces of their Majesties if I betray my best friend?"

"Your best friend is being pressured to hand over the Lady Guinevere as a trophy of war."

Lancelot takes a long swig at his ale, sighs and gently places it back on the polished table.

"Long live King Arthur. Come, Al, we have work to do."

Without another word, he pushes back the stool that he has been sitting on, draws himself up, and leaves.

Ch. 13 The Impossible Exploit

Lancelot and Al are again walking some distance from the castle, the only place safe to talk about their mission.

The knight has used his proximity with Galahaut to question him about the security measures, put into place to protect the magical spectre.

Using the angle; that if someone had thought to kidnap the Lady Dena, then their true interest would likely be to ransom her for it.

"It's impossible," he shakes his golden locks, "it is locked in a tower, and the only staircase is manned twenty-four hours per day, with four guards on every landing, and there are three landings."

"So there are twelve guards." Al calculates.

"Yes, and the staircase is only wide enough for one, maybe two people. There is no way that we could get up to the tower, never mind down again. It's just impossible." He sighs heavily.

"I'll just have to send a message that it cannot be done."

"Maybe?" Al seems to be lost in a parallel world of his own.

"Al!"

"What? Oh yes. Wait, if it's impossible to get up to the tower and down again, from the inside, what about the outside?"

"It would be impossible; no normal man could manage to do that."

"But what about if they were acrobats?"

"Acrobats?"

"Yes, acrobats."

"And you happen to know some acrobats that are also thieves?"

"As it happens, I think that I do."

"And do they have names these acrobat, thieves?"

"There leader is called Faron, and another is named Michael, the last one, who's really nice, don't know 'is name."

"And where might we find them?"

"I can find them."

"Are they on the island?"

"No, but they're only a few hours away from the port."

"And you'd trust them?"

Al takes a moment to reflect before responding.

"Well, we don't have that much to lose, do we?"

"I guess that you're right. Okay, we leave on the first boat tomorrow morning. "

Ch. 14 The Unholy Alliance

The tavern is dark, hot, smoky and tangy with the sweat of the tosspots.

They snake their way through the crowded room.

Al recognises Faron from his poster and the company of Michael and the tall guy.

They are well known in the town, and it hadn't taken them long to locate them.

Faron is in the midst of entertaining the public with some tale of his bedding the beautiful, young chambermaid of some foreign princess, from an imprecise kingdom, somewhere in Europe.

"An so's there I am, goin' up to the royal chamber …" As Al appears out of the shadows, he loses the thread of his story.

Following his gaze, Michael jumps up off of his stool, "What the …?"

The scene is further galvanised by the appearance of Lancelot.

"So this is the famous Faron, is it?"

"Ay, good eve, sire." Although the knight is hooded and his face, all but impossible to make out, his stature and all too visible sword, make him a person, clearly to be reckoned with.

The fact that he is travelling with the 'kidnappee', he, who was kidnapped, does little to calm the nerves of the three criminals.

"Come gentlemen, we have business to discuss."

And without a second glance, he turns and threads his way back out to the clear, cold, evening air.

They had not succeeded to leave as early as planned, as the Lord Galahaut had insisted on interviewing Al about their capture and subsequent flight to freedom.

The squire having had the time to reflect, had invented a fairly convincing story.

And, even if it was a little lacking in certain important details, the fact that he succeeded to escape and liberate the princess, it was enough to satisfy the sovereign.

Moments later, the three culprits ooze out of the inn door. They must have been too scared to ignore the big, scary looking man's order, but are still very unsure just what to expect.

… Until the showman awakens.

"So you's okay boy? Did 'er 'ighness get back to the castle safety then?"

Al is quite shocked by Faron's friendly attitude.

"Yes, yes, she's home and safe. No thanks to you." He cannot help but adding.

"Yeh, well, we wus jus' doin' a job. No 'arm done." And, strangely enough, he smiles and goes to walk away.

"I have not dismissed you yet." The knight takes on a commanding tone.

"Yes, yes of course sire, and to 'oom might I be 'avin' the pleasure to be addressing?"

"The man that might either choose to slit your throat, or fill your pocket with gold."

"We really do not mean to harm, her ladyship."

"I know that you didn't." Al responds openly to the tall one.

"None of us did."

"You said that you wanted to kill me." He is not so forgiving towards Michael.

"Tha' wus jus' t' scare ya' into behavin'".

"Should I run him through, what do you think?" Now it is Lancelot's turn to play cat and mouse.

"And jus' what do we 'ave to do to have our pockets filled with gold?"

Faron, the deal maker, has not forgotten the offer of employment.

"This is a very delicate matter, and if you, so much as breath a word of this enterprise to anyone, I will, run you through."

"In our line of business, we've no place for blob-tales. A loose tongue is a cut-tongue, if you gets *my* drift."

"It's one night's work, and there's silver for it."

" 'Ere's me handband," he offers to shake on the deal. Lancelot accepts, and the agreement is sealed.

"You will come to the island tomorrow night, you will need ropes and irons. You will be climbing down the side of a building. A please try and be a little discrete."

"Jus' one more thing, sire."

"What is it?"

"We would do to 'ave a few chinkers, like for travelling money."

Lancelot digs into his leather pouch and extracts some coins, which he drops in Faron's, dirty, outstretched palm.

"We'll be seein' ya'."

And the three stooges, melt quickly into the blackness.

"Do you think that we'll see them again?" Al is less convinced than when he suggested the idea to the knight.

"That's why I offered them silver." Lancelot smiles, and pats the knave on the shoulder.

"Let's go and hunt up some supper."

Ch. 15 Theft

It must be admitted that Galahaut's castle was not well defended.

After all, it is situated on a rather small island, only 33 miles in length and 13 miles in width, so it would seem unlikely that anyone would risk attacking or robbing the royal household.

As such, it isn't difficult for the three miscreants to gain entrance, even with their unlikely tackle.

They discover Al, waiting for them in the shadows. It is already late afternoon.

"This way up to the battlements." They climb the steep, stone steps leading to the parapet.

"We'll need somewhere to wait until it's gettin a bit dimpse. And then, until it's safe to leave."

"The scrow'll be well covered tonight." The tall one, who's name, Al discovered is Duncan, is looking up at the sky, and nodding his head in satisfaction.

Al points out the tower, which, although it has a door leading into it from their level, has also two guards to protect the locked door, on this side.

Lancelot has informed them that there are likewise, two other guards on the other side.

However, the plan is not to enter by any door. There is a window in the tower, which being so very high up, has been created to be unusually wide.

The logic was, that as it looks out over the bay, it could be used as a lookout post. Giving the sentry a full panoramic view of anyone arriving on the island from the mainland.

It is through this window, that Michael, being the smallest, would hope to enter the circular piece, and retrieve the treasure.

Al knew of a turret room that he led them to, before bidding them, the best of luck, and returning to his regular duties, hoping that his absence had not been overly noticed.

The rest of the night's adventures he only hears the details of, some moons after the event, as retold by Faron.

Standing before a blazing fire, in a dusty tavern, in between several glasses of mead.

"So there we are, jus' the three of us, against a hundred castle guards.

We waited 'til it wus getting' dark.

We waz feeling a little sloomy, a bit sleepy, hangin' around.

But's we had a job to do, and 'sheart we promised, no matter the risk.

We sneaks out of the turret room, draggin' our gear as quietly as a huntin'fox.

The plan is get 'round to the back o' the tower, which fo' an ordinary man would be impossible.

But we ain't no ordinary men.

We climbs over the parapet.

Then usin' the embrasures, the gaps in the crenellations to swing along the outside of the wall, we gets to the back o' the tower.

The guards don't see nor hear nothin'. Silent as owls we waz.

I then climbs back onto the rampart, checkin' that all is clear.

Duncan and Michael climbs up to me bringin' the rope and grapple.

The eyethurl, is quite a big window, but still too small for me, and no chance for Duncan. Mikey bein' small and scraggly is jus' the right size.

Duncan hurls the hook, but misses the first time, he has to pull it so it falls over the wall, so not land of the ground, and not make any noise.

We hears the soldiers talkin'.

What if they think to walk round to where we are?

What if someone might see us?

We'd be fish in a barrel?

There'd be no-where to run.
We'd 'ave to fight.
A fight to the death.
Against heavily armed and trained soldiers.
We'd 'ave to fight, fight to survive.
And we would, 'cus we're no strangers t' danger.
But … nobody came.
We breaved a sigh of relief, we'd not 'ave t' kill no one t'night.
Duncan throws the hook again.
Too high?
No, no it slides down the empty space of the window, and blocks onto the sill.
He tugs to make sure that it'll hold.
It moves.
We holds our breath.
It stops, it clamps onto the stone ledge.
I grabs the rope, and we pulls it real tight.
Michael shinnies up the cord, like a squirrel after nuts.
And disappears into the hole.
He knows where to look to get the sceptre.
It takes no time at all before he's stickin' 'is noggin' out and givin' us the wave.
I've letted go of the rope, and was ready for the most important catch o' me life.
By the way 'es holdin' it, I can see that it'll be heavy.
I make the sign, and he drops it towards me.
It falls bloody fast.
But I'm ready.
I catches it, no trouble.
But it's so weighty I also drops it.
Duncan gets his hand around part of it, and then it's safe.

Mikey then pulls the hook off and throws it back over the battlements.

I grabs the rope and wait for the pull as it reaches the bottom of its fall.

Suddenly I'm being tugged towards an embrasure, but Duncan grabs me round the middle and stops me being thrown over into the black emptiness o' the night.

We then link our arms to make a square net and Michael lets hi'self drop from the keep.

As professional, world known acrobats, we catches him with ease.

We wraps the sceptre in some cloth, and attach some rope to the ends.

Duncan swings it over 'is shoulders and we climbs back over the parapet, and makes our way back t' the turret room.

There we hide the rope and the prized rod.

And then, job done, we goes back to the local tidliwink for some food and a big jubbe of hum.

Sure, the sentry stops us goin' out, but we's not carryin' nothin', so no trouble.

And that, gentlemen, is 'ow we, Faron and company, stole the famous Uffington sceptre, made by Merlin himself, from the most guarded donjon of King Galahaut."

Yes, it makes a great story.

However, it might have been a little prudent to have not starting sharing this tale, until Lancelot and Al had made it safely to Camelot.

Ch. 16 The Ambush

Al would have felt happier to have left immediately after he had retrieved the sceptre from the turret room.

He had waited until the cock had crowed, before hunting out the precious package.

That way, it would not seem suspicious, his wondering around the castle.

He then stowed it with their riding gear and returned to his normal duties.

Lancelot had decided that they would leave after the midday meal, after letting it be known that he had decided to return to his own keep, to check up on events of the past weeks.

And so now, they are back in the southern road, returning, with the spoils, not of war, but of theft.

It is early evening and they are enjoying a gentle swaying of the horse's movement.

Each, lost in their own thoughts, relaxed, drowsy, taking maybe just too little attention to their surroundings.

"Wooooo!"

A dart flies out of the trees ahead. Heading straight for Al's head.

"What?!" he cries out in shock and surprise, as he does his best to duck and avoid the shrieking missile.

At the speed that it comes at him, his dulled reflexes are not going to be quick enough.

He braces for the impact … but it doesn't hit.

For it is not an arrow, it is a bird. A long-eared owl, is continuing its flight, it only brushes against his face, and is disappearing back into the shadows of the little forest, but not from the direction from which it came.

It takes a moment for Al to clear his vision of the orange headed, yellow eyed creature, that, all but pierced his right eye.

The event had fully woken them up.

"Stop!" Lancelot calls out a warning.

Al looks to where he is pointing and sees something moving the bushes.

Without a second's hesitation, he flings himself down onto his horse's neck.

The whiz of the arrow passes inches from where his neck was situated only seconds before.

He hears, rather than sees, Lancelot jumping down from his horse. Using it as a mighty shield, against the archer or archers hiding in the heavy cover.

"Come out you cowards and test your steal against a true knight."

Al is now, likewise on foot, protected by the solid flesh of his steed.

Not wanting to stay unprotected, he digs into the saddle bags, and fishes out his master's spare sword.

It is big and heavy, but also excellently balanced, which makes it much easier to handle than one would otherwise imagine.

Looking over the head of the horse's mane, he watches as three men run out of the shadows. Their faces are hidden by thick scarves.

They encircle Lancelot and bare down on him from three sides.

He points his sword horizontally and spins round like a mad spindle. Although the aim of this one, is not to gather the yarn together, but to keep the men at bay.

Clearly this can only a very short-term strategy, he surely cannot keep up the momentum for very long. His energy will out, and the vultures will have their prey.

Al appears from behind his horse yielding the impressive weapon.
"You ever picked up a sword before, me lad?" One of the assailants notices the action and turns his attention to the youth.

In all this excitement and danger, there has been a niggling doubt in Al's mind. A doubt that has expressed itself enough for the experienced fighter to perceive.

On seeing the three figures arrive, his first thought is that Faron and his company have thought to augment their profits and steal the sceptre.

On hearing this strange voice, part of him experiences a massive feeling of relief.

At least they had not betrayed him.

He advances towards the robber.

Now he must make a decision, stay on Lancelot, and ignore the boy, hoping that he is really no danger, or deal with the runt, and leave the knight to the other two.

Al, scared but determined continues towards the burly adversary.

Now, not having much choice, he turns to the hesitant squire and lances a heavy blow.

Trusting his reflexes, Al moves to block the swinging sword, but hasn't been able to take into account the sheer force of the attack.

Although he does succeed to protect himself from the sharp metal, the thrust is strong enough to knock him down.

Lancelot has taken advantage in only having two assailants, to stop his spin and to engage them both.

To begin with, he is doing well and his already injured one of the men.

Unfortunately, he has not noticed that a forth has appeared from out of the shadows.

The forth robber creeps up and bashes the knight, savagely on the back of his head.

Lancelot slumps down, all the spirit knocked out of him. Little more than a raggedy doll.

"Come, let's get it."

"No you don't." Al is back on his feet. Only this time, he has not one but four opponents to deal with.

"You see to 'im, and I'll get the stick."

The other robber goes towards the youth. Through the scarf, one could see an evil smile curling his thick lips.

"This aren't to take too long."

All is clearly lost. He doesn't even know how he might defend himself against this one seasoned fighter, stopping all four, that is surely impossible.

"I wouldn'st be thinking o' doin' tha' y' whiteliver theow."

From the corner of an eye, he perceives more figures appear, who are taking on the other robbers. There is no time to think more than, 'at least I've just one to deal with.'

He then readies himself for the attack.

'He believes that you don't know how to use a sword, let will be to your advantage.'

It feels as if there is someone else with him, coaching him, advising him.

'Let him come to you and then attack with an axe cut."

Not knowing what else to do, he accepts to follow this inner voice.

The guy comes slowly forward, the cat will take a few moments pleasure before killing and devouring the mouse.

Everyone has the right to a little recreation, from time to time.

Al, heart racing, scared, yet excited, screams and runs towards the human feline.

He is screaming, running and raising his sword, ready to drop and cleave the head into two.

If anything, amused, the older man stops, easily leans back on his right foot for support, and raises his sword to fend off the naïve attack.

Only it doesn't arrive.

Not there.

In mid swing, Al's sword has veered away from the head. Curved a wide arc under the other's sword arm, and chopped him on the right hip.

Although the thick leather jerkin must have absorbed a fair amount of the blow, it is clear that he won't be troubling anyone, anymore this day.

Having miraculously downed his opponent, he now has the time to look round and take in the scene.

The other three bandits, now being confronted by an equal number of combatants, and seeing that their forth will not only be unable to help, but has been bested, have lost their thirst to fight.

They now circle their wounded colleague, drag him back to his feet, and retreat back into the forest.

He runs to his prostrate master to see if he is still of this world.

But he need not of worried, Lancelot is already coming round.

"I s'pose that you could be thankin' us f' savin' ya'."

Al turns to his saviors.

Thank you, Faron, Michael and …?"

"Duncan McCloud, at your service." The tall one smiles and bows.

"And you will be thanked in a more material fashion when we arrive in Camelot, as promised," Lancelot is now back on his feet.

"The handband of a knight, that's givi' y' word." Faron smiles.

"Come, let's get out of here, who knows if there might be other surprises." They mount up.

Al is tremendously pleased, if not a little surprised that Faron and company just happened to be close by, and to save him from, what would surely have been, a particularly unpleasant lesson in swordplay.

He reflects that they would have been coming also to Camelot to receive their payment for helping in the theft of the sceptre.

However, his relief proves to be particularly short-lived.

Lancelot turns round to him with a rather puzzled look.

"Now, where is it that we are supposed to be going to?"

Ch. 17 Hail the Conquering Hero

They are riding; Al, Lancelot, and the good friar, who seemed well informed of their arrival and was waiting for them outside of the city.

The three acrobats will enter discretely, separately.

Lancelot is wearing his helmet even though the visor is up, he is riding with his eyes closed. It seems that he is coping poorly with the strong sunlight.

Even if he cannot remember anything else, fortunately he is still quite capable to ride.

The hot, dry breeze carries the cries of the crowd, for a crowd, indeed there is, cheering and shouting.

"Welcome, champion, welcome champion ….", over and over again.

Maybe it is the cries of the people, but the hero reacts and opens his eyes and peeks out into this seemingly, new world.

They are surrounded by excited peasants, they are about to enter a walled town, raising their eyes, they can just make out the ramparts of the medieval castle.

"Smile and wave, smile and wave," the wording and the repetition reminds him of something, but Al cannot place the phrase that the friar, riding a mule, is shouting into Lancelot's left ear.

"What?" Lancelot shouts back, he seems quite confused.

"You're a hero, so please could you try acting like one," and then adds, as a sort of afterthought, "and yes, before you think to ask, it's me." Al understands that the priest is coaching his master as how to behave and that he is indeed the friar Brendan.

"I suppose that I am starting to get used to your multiple incarnations. "

"And I, yours," the two 'allies', smile easily at each other. Al is now a little lost with the conversation, but takes the interaction to be a possible good sign.

"You are recovered, sire?"

Lancelot turns to his right. The handsome, young man, riding a stubby, brown pony, smiles up at him.

"Yes, yes, I seem to be recovered, but ….," the sentence trails off, and they continue awhile in silence.
" ..Only, I cannot remember anything," he finally admits.

"Nothing, sire?" Al is beginning to feel particularly concerned. He had hoped that the knight's memory loss would only be short term, but it has now lasted for almost a full day.

"Not even my own name," he concludes uncomfortably.

"You received a nasty bump to the head, I trust that all will right itself with time. I will supply you with such knowledge as I have." Al is doing his best to find the supportive words that might ease Lancelot's discomfort.

He sighs as his master nods his head in acknowledgement, he seems slightly relieved, and then turns back to his spiritual guide.

"I don't remember anything of this person's life."

"It seems that you have recently been victim to a nasty blow to the cranium."

"That information is not particularly helpful."

"If you have been injured, and are suffering from amnesia, then that is the reality that you will need to deal with. And remember, 'smile and wave'."

The victory procession passes through the high arch that delimits the countryside from the protected city.

The streets are thronged with masses of cheering people.

They continue to weave their way through the narrow
streets, up, into the castle keep.

Another stone wall is passed through, and they arrive in
the courtyard of the castle, itself.

Ch. 18 A Royal Welcome

As they approach the courtyard, one cannot help but notice the increasing presence of more and more guards. There is also a marked improvement in the quality of the clothes and presentation of the townspeople.

By the time that the three enter the enclosed space, there are almost no more peasants, quite a lot of middle and upper-class citizens, and many guards, and, not really surprising, knights.

Now, the two supporting riders fall back, and Lancelot is alone to approach the royal podium.

The king and queen are already standing, both beautifully dressed; in elegance and in luxury.

The king is wearing a long-embroidered tunic, with a red velvet cloak edged with some type of animal fur, decorated tan leather boots, a golden crown, and many rings.

Al, now having nothing better to do, takes in all the details of the scene being played out before him.

The queen, is clearly most pleased to see her knight.

All the violence and anger that he can still remember of when she threw him out, (from Lancelot's memories), must have faded, and her old love, restored.

He has never seen her look so pleased to see him.

Unfortunately, the king, didn't seem to be as pleased as all that.

Of course, he is smiling, he is here to congratulate the conquering hero, for the wonderful act he had just accomplished.

Even if the poor knight would be rather more comfortable to know exactly what it was that he had just done.

'I really must find the time to remind him,' the squire reflects.

However, what he has just done, is to Arthur, less important than what he had done in the past.

For, even if he, doesn't know or remember anything about his own history,
Al remembers everything about his life before he lost his memory.

Maybe he would do his master a service to remind him of some other, less glorious exploits, that have happened in the past.

Things specifically to do with his relationship with the king, or even more so, with the king's wife, the Lady Guinevere.

For he knows the king, through his friends, servants of the castle, he knows him all too well.

He knows that the king can be happy but doesn't always choose to show it.

He also knows that he can be irritated or angry, but choses to smile and act like everything is fine.

At times, during a feast, when one of his lower vassals, having slightly over-indulged of the free-flowing alcohol, would approach his lord, and say something, rather inappropriate.

The king would just smile, and say something inconsequential, pat him in a rather patronising way, on the back, and propel him away from his group of intimates.

And that is how the king, is looking at the hero, now.

But before he has time for any more reflections, the knight's horse is brought before the royal family.

Al, watching from behind follows Lancelot's approach and from the position of his head, what he is looking at.

For it is only when he gets really close to the podium that he notices that there is another member of the royal family.

Sitting demurely, on a small throne, is the princess.

No, not just any princess, his princess, the princess Angelique.

His heart skips a beat. Here she is, Angelique, beautiful as always; fiery hair, cat's eyes.

 "My subjects, this is a moment of celebration." The king proclaims and the crowd roars.

"Our noble son has returned to us, after so many months of self-imposed exile."

The queen, gives her husband an evil stare.

"But not empty handed. He has brought with him, one of the greatest prizes of all England, the Uffington sceptre. Made by Merlin himself, to block Mordred's charms, given over to the traitorous king Galahaut."

Al is listening to the speech but must have also drifted off on another thought tangent.

He suddenly realises that Arthur. has stopped speaking and is looking at Lancelot. Actually, everyone is looking at him.

Only is seems that he has absolutely no idea what he might be expected to say.

There is a movement in the crowd, Al forces his way through.

"If I might be of service, m'lord?"

The disaster has to be avoided, what the reaction might be, if they found out that the knight had lost all memory of who he is, is impossible to guess.

"That would be a really good idea." He smiles at Al, the relief clearly perceivable in his voice.

"Here,", Al pulls a wrapped object from out of the saddle bag, and gives it carefully to him. Then catches the hero's regard, looks to the thing, and then towards the king.

Quick enough on the uptake, Lancelot offers it ceremoniously to his liege.

The king gently takes the mummified rod and slowly unwraps it, the crowd waits in total silence.

The sceptre is a beautiful intricate affaire. Made up of three twisted, twisting strands of metal.

Likely to be gold and silver, but what the third might be, is not obvious. There is a great diamond at the tip, but also other gems are part of the design.

Al has not seen this magnificent object, until today, it has always been hidden under swathes of cloth. He, like the crowd, marvels at the beautifully wrought sceptre.

The king holds up the trophy in triumph.

The crowd roars.

The crowd applauds their all-powerful king.

Al looks up to his master and notices that his posture has become unstable, he grabs hold of the horse's neck, in an effort not to fall down, and perhaps irritate the king even more.

He slips, and falls, Al succeeds to block him as he slides out of his saddle.

And with the help of several, attentive soldiers, manages to ease him onto the cobbled ground, without further incident.

Ch. 19 The Necessary

They bring a cart and gently place the prostrate knight onto the pile of straw, lining the inner, wooden structure.

"He received a blow to the head, protecting the sceptre, on his journey to return it to your Majesty."

The friar responds to Arthur's inquiry as to what has just occurred.

"Take him to his chambers," he seems almost dismissive of his knight's plight.

Al is conflicted, he would wish to accompany Lancelot to his bed chamber, but as his squire, his first responsibility must be to look after their horses.

Yet again, the aging monk comes to his rescue.

"I will see that the horses are appropriately taken care of, you stay with Lancelot."

Gladly, he hands over the reins, and jumps into the back of the cart.

Having supervised his master being carried upstairs, and being safely deposited on the bed, Al goes to find his own sleeping quarters.

He has been assigned a hard bed in a room with three other castle employees.

The room is small, stuffy, smelly and his bunk is being used as extra storage space for the affairs of the others.

He feels a heavy exhaustion weighing on him but cannot think to start clearing the bed, nor feel comfortable in this unclean and clustered, chamber.

So he grabs his tack and heaves it back up to the knight's chamber.

He has noticed that there is a large alcove, curtained off from the rest of the room. It might be a dressing space for a female occupant.

He is happy to discover a chaise longue, plonks himself on it, throws a blanket that he has borrowed from his official bed over his still clothed body, and drops off into a deep sleep.

When the knight awakes, it is already quite dark. Al wakes up to the sounds of his master sitting up on the side of the bed.

For the moment he doesn't make any effort to move, he can easily see what is happening from his narrow bed.

Especially as there is no light in this area and someone has lit several candles in the other part of the room.

Clearly enough so he can see Lancelot as he moves 'round.

He wanders over to the washing bowl, there is a water jug, filled and the rough towel, carefully, folded.

"Hello, is anybody there?" He calls out, surely hoping that someone is in hearing distance.

Al, still half asleep, forces himself into motion.

What his master clearly didn't expect, was the sound of something heavy, dropping onto the floor, from a dark corner, of the room.

"What the ...?"

"My apologies, m'lord, you surprised me," Al appears from the shadows, it is obvious that he has also benefited from a free moment to grab a little shut eye.

"Are you feeling better, sire?" He is now even more concerned about the knight's state of health.

"I need to find a toilet."

"There's a pot under the bed."

"A pot won't do."

"Then please follow me." Al, having friends serving in the castle, has had, on many occasions the opportunity to familiarise himself with the inner geography of the building.

He leads them out of the room and along several corridors and then, indicates a small door.

The knight, seems slightly confused on entering the toilet chamber, but much more relieved by the time he exits.

The sleep and execution of nature's needs seem to have awakened his body and spirits. "Do you think that you might succeed to find something for us to eat?"

"The banquet in your honour will be served shortly, there will surely be more than enough to appease your hunger, sire." Al informs him.

"Great, but why do you keep and calling me sire?" He truly seems to not understand.

"Because you are a knight, and a brave and glorious knight, at that." Maybe he can get him to remember something.

"But I don't remember I don't even remember your name." This is not improving.

"That's okay, you can call me Al." A vague memory of something invades his consciousness.

Lancelot also seems distracted. "Are you feeling bad again?" The squire is seriously concerned.

"No, no, it's quite alright," he returns back to the present. "And another thing, I don't remember anything that I have done."

"No, matter, your noble exploits are song all over the kingdom." He is still hoping to sound reassuring.

Lancelot stops and looks sternly at the squire, who continues.

"You succeeded to steal the magical sceptre from King Galahaut."

"And why is it magical?" Al, shakes his head, more for himself, than for anything else.

"It was created by to Merlin block all magical attacks. It was a gift given as a gesture of eternal peace and friendship."

"And who gave it to him?"

"Why the king, of course."

"The same king that I have just stolen it for?"

"Exactly."

"But why?" 'It's like talking to a child'.

"It seems that he is amassing a secret army to mount a surprise attack on Camelot."

"Did we see any signs of this secret army?" Fair question.

"It wouldn't be very secret if we could." Obvious answer.

"Good point." 'Yes, it is.'

"But why attack Camelot anyway?" The younger stops and takes a breath.

"That is what I believe, is termed as politics."

"Sounds crazy to me." 'Does one have to totally erase everything that one has ever been taught, to be able to understand the obvious?'

"Sounds like it's time to dress you for your feast." Al is starting to tire in his role as preceptor.

"Sounds like a plan."

And off they go.

Ch. 20 The Banquet

Lancelot is at the entrance of a great banquet room, Al
has directed him to the doorway, but doesn't choose to
enter.

Unknown to most, there are several vantage points where
one can conceal oneself, yet clearly see and hear all that
is happening in the great hall.

Al steals a chunk of meal and a lump of bread and installs
himself behind a latticed screen.

He doesn't have the habit to spy on his betters, but he is
concerned for his master, and feels it necessary to keep
track on what is going on.

The honoured guest enters the noisy room, and slowly
makes his way towards the high-table at the rear, a wave
of silence precedes him.

By the time he arrives in front of the haute nobility, the
room has frozen in both sound and movement.

He bows towards his liege, his lady and finally, to the
angel.

"I trust that you are recovered, m'lord." It is the lady of the house that breaks the silence.

Being the first to speak, to take control of the situation, has always been her domain.

"I slept well, m'lady. I apologise for my display of weakness. I trust that it was not taken as any sign of disrespect."

"There is no need to trouble yourself about us feeling any disrespect." It is the king, himself that has chosen to interject.

There is something in that look and tone of voice that rings a bell.

A thousand flashes of standing in front of his father, his mother at his side, both of them looking sadly at him.

It is if Lancelot is about to be told off for something, but now? Here? After having done just as he was asked.

Al is asking himself, 'what is his problem?

He's the mighty king. We've gotten him the fancy, magic stick that he wanted.

'Can't anyone ever get it right, in this kingdom, or any other?

'Okay, let's just watch them continue on with this crazy charade.'

"Thank you, my lord." Lancelot bows again.

"Come, sit between us," the queen gestures to an empty seat, between her and Angelique.

The queen is dressed in various shades of red, fine silks, layered and heavily embroidered.

The princess, sports a deceivingly simple looking, green velvet dress, ornamented with yellow, silk ribbons. The effect, due to the red hair and green eyes, is, undeniably stunning.

Looking lost for something neutral to say, all the knight can think of is …

"Your ribbons match the colour of my tunic," for indeed, he is wearing a top of exactly the same colour.

"'T'was my Lady Marion, that chose them for me," she smiles at him.

Al smiles to himself, it didn't take much persuading of his past, fellow tavern co-worker, to get her to suggest to the young lady to choose the yellow ribbons.

If he could get the two to fall in love, then Lancelot would be free of his infatuation of Queen Guinevere, and the danger of another *slip* might be avoided.

However, things are not really so simple, he is, for reasons particularly unclear to himself, not totally sure that he would wish for this particular scheme to work.

Anyway, it seems to be the best idea that he can come up with at this time, so that's the way things are going to be played.

"Then she chose well," the gallant knight continues, but before she has the time to respond, the 'other woman', addresses him.

"You have succeeded to regain your name and the respect of our people."

"But not yet, that of the king," he responds, in a whisper that Al more guesses than hears.

"There are things that might never be forgiven, nor forgotten. He has accepted for you to return; he has welcomed you, this banquet is thrown in your honour, it would be unwise to hope for more.

After-all, it is for you to accept, humbly, any scraps that he deigns to throw you." Her voice is little more than the hush of a quiet breeze.

"You are, as always, as *sage*, as you are beautiful," he smiles softly, as he makes a slight bow.

'Not again, 'as sage as you are beautiful' Why would he still be trying to seduce her?' Al sighs heavily, he will really have to work hard with his Cupid's bow.

"So, tell me," she continues in a louder, public voice, "what new adventures do you have planned, now that you have succeeded the impossible?"

"I will conquer something much more difficult than that."

He holds his breath, what might his knight, who knows not even who he is, choose as another conquest?

"Do tell us," she goads him. Several people, close by, stop to hear his response.

"I will conquer the heart of the fairest maiden in the land."

' 'S'heart, he'll be hung before daybreak!'

There is an icy silence that cuts through the room.

It is more than clear that Lancelot has realised that he has made an enormous gaff, but exactly what, he surely doesn't know.

He immediately takes a deep breath, and before anyone can react further, he succeeds to add, with a wolfish grin …

"… that is not otherwise taken." and scoops up her hand, and bows again, to softly kiss the smooth, white skin.

Al lets out the longest of breaths, but how will she respond?

"Such a noble quest, of the heart," she smiles back.

The young man crosses himself and promises to light a candle to the virgin the very next Sunday.

From his vantage point, he follows Lancelot's gaze, as he looks over the queen's shoulder. He only has to glance across to catch the fierce expression, hidden behind the placid smile, of the king.

One only had to look into those pinhole, pupils to gage the extent of his rage.

Was it the first remark of capturing the most beautiful maiden, or was it the second phrase and the gesture of the kiss on the hand, that has evoked this intense reaction?

He can easily image how Lancelot must feel puzzled, and not just a little concerned to have so upset his powerful host.

However, it is clear that he still chooses to steal away his attention from the afore mentioned shark and look to the reaction of his personal prey.

Much to his surprise, turning, he finds that Angelique is in an animated conversation, with her neighbour to her right.

"Have you lost something?"

In the complex mix of thoughts and emotions, he seems to have forgotten the existence of the one person, that he is in direct interaction with.

"My apologies M'dame, I thought that I heard your daughter asking me something?"

"My daughter? Sire, why would you refer to Angelique as my daughter? She is his daughter; do you think me old enough to have a daughter of her age?"

She sounds shocked, even horrified.

'Oh my God, he's done it again.' And yet, she doesn't look angry, actually, she seems quite amused. He then realises that she is playing with him.

He also realises, that somewhere, that this is quite an intimate game. One would only risk this type of intercourse with someone that one was safely close too.

"To call her your sister, although more likely, would be technically inaccurate.

I only referred to her, as your daughter, in the general term, as the daughter of your husband."

'He's so good with words, if only I could speak to women like that. In front of a maiden, I can do nothing more than stutter.'

He ruefully reflects, in total admiration of the knight's ability to twist out of the most awful errors.

Again, he smiles that warm, winning, seductive smile.

Also, again, he is seducing her. Here, in public, sitting almost on the king's lap, in front of everyone, this is more than insane, it is suicidal.

And yet, there is worse. How can he possibly succeed to capture Angelique, when he is still Hell bent of bedding her own step-mother?

Suddenly, he is seen to react; he sits bolt upright, his head jerks back and up, something now has hit him.

Like an eight-wheeled, out of control, cannon carrying cart, straight between the eyes.

Lancelot gently raises from his seat and walks towards the king.

"Your majesty?" He waits politely for the monarch to turn to him.

Al holds his breath, 'what now?'

"If it please your majesty, during the recuperation of the sceptre, I received a heavy blow to the head.

Which explains my behaviour over the past hours and days. If I have said or done anything that might have displeased you, please accept my most humble apologies." Again, the boy, can exhale his tension.

He waits for a moment to give the other the time to reply, but none comes, so he continues.

"I am again feeling that maybe I might have another malaise, and so would ask your permission to withdraw."

"This banquet has been thrown in your honour, Sir Lancelot. To acknowledge your courage and valour. Please take your seat, you cannot leave before we offer you a toast in your name."

The knight nods and returns to his seat.

The king stands and almost immediately the room becomes still.

"Sir Lancelot, Lancelot of the lake, brother in arms, my adopted son, and knight of the round table. We have terribly missed you these past months.

We understand that you had demons to fight, demons that you have had to face alone, demons that took you from our bosom.

But you have faced, fought, and set to flight those demons. And now you have returned, bolder and braver than ever before.

Sir Lancelot, your loss, has disappointed us. I pray to your God, that you never have to disappoint us again, and that you will stay with us, and once again, you can call Camelot your home.

To Lancelot!"

And the crowd roars. "Lancelot, Lancelot, Lancelot." Goblets are raised and drinks are drunk.

Arthur salutes Lancelot, a gesture that should have filled him with pride and joy, but remains sadly empty. He and they both know that this is just a show for the public.

So, now he must speak, must continue the farce, must play the conquering hero, must acknowledge the salute.

He raises slowly to his feet, all eyes on the conquering hero.

"Thank you, thank you. High praise, as it comes from the greatest king that has ever lived. A king that has already unified all of southern England.

All I do, and all that I have done, has only been for God and king. Let us drink to the king. King Arthur!"

'If they want a show, then here's your show.' Al smiles in admiration of his master.

They drink to Arthur, their king.

"Unfortunately, during the last battles, I received some injuries to the head, which still trouble me. So, I must allow myself to leave you now. Enjoy the rest of the banquet. Eat, drink and be merry."

"Lancelot, Lancelot, Lancelot!" They chant, and drink, and chant and drink.

The noise and movement allow him to withdraw without having to trouble himself to take his leave correctly, with either of the women.

By the time that he takes to arrive at the great door, Al, is already waiting for him. He then escorts the exhausted looking knight, in silence, back to their safe, quiet, solitary chamber.

Ch. 21 An Unpleasant Interview

They do not speak as they return to Lancelot's chamber, Al realises that he has misread the condition of his master, he is not tired, in fact it has become clear that the knight is in a foul mood.

Once safely installed, he dispatches Al, to go and seek out the rotund friar.

In that smooth, unobtrusive fashion that only servants and servers have, he floats, semi-invisibly, back into the banquet to seek out Friar Brendan,

It is not so difficult to locate the spiritual advisor.

The holy man has the roasted leg of some, quite large animal in one hand and a large goblet of some, presumably alcoholic drink in the other.

He is singing a less than saintly sea shanty at the top of his voice and is clearly having rather a good time.

"Father?" Al is a little uncomfortable interrupting this joyous moment.

"What? Oh, it's you, my son. Come, come and join us in a round."

"I, I, I, I c'c'cannot," his nervousness expresses itself in his stutter.

"Oh yes, you are now Lancelot's squire. So, you cannot join us, not to worry, God's speed. Alain." It seems that he has already forgotten that Al approached him for something.

"Sir Lancelot is sick, h'he has a'a'asked f'for you." He splutters out, as best as he can.

"Oh? Yes, Lancelot, Faron, yes, I have to go to him." He takes a bite of the meat and swallows it down with a great swig from the tankard.

'Faron? What could this possibly have to do with Faron?' But before he has the opportunity to reflect more on this enigma, Brendan is on his feet, and they are exiting the banquet.

Al would very much like to question the father, as to the meaning behind his last statement, but he was much too concerned that his master might do something unwise if they tarried too long.

He imagined that the knight would be either sobbing in pain or vivid in a blazing fit of anger.

Instead, he finds himself on his knees, praying, clutching a heavy, silver crucifix,

"My child, you wish for absolution?" The priest offers to help.

"No, I fucking want to kill you!"

"My child?"

"Fuck the 'my child', crap! What's this pile of shit, you've gotten me into?"

"I'm sorry, I am not following you."

The holy man then turns and smiles gently at Al, "it seems that the hit on the head was worse than I thought. Maybe you would like to go and find yourself some food while I try and sooth your master."

Al looks towards Lancelot. "Yes, yes, that would be a good idea. The good friar and I have things to discuss," the knight concurs.

"I, I, I shall be in the k'k'kitchens, if you should need me." He still seems slightly unsure to leave Lancelot, in the state that he is in.

"Enjoy your meal," it is a gentle command.

"Good evening, masters," he gives a slight bow and leaves, softly closing the door as he goes.

And so, he descends to the kitchens, where he feeds off much more than common food.

Much, much, more indeed.

Ch. 22 New World in the Morning

It seems that he had slept badly, he has never slept so late. The usual breakfast, being served between six and eight has already been cleared away.

Now all that is offered is bread and ale, which doesn't help him to shake off his clearly, depressed mood.

Al has just appeared with a slab of venison, aware that Lancelot had eaten little the preceding evening, he presumed that he would be especially hungry, and had sweet talked someone in the kitchens to giving up this little prize.

Pleasantly surprised, and even a little impressed by this feat, he inquires how he managed it.

"I grew up here, in Camelot, I know almost everyone that serves here, in the castle, we all went to school, played and fooled around, together."

"So, if I wanted something done, or a message given to someone, then you would know how to do that?"

"When you might need, such a service, m'lord, I would be honoured to see that it gets done."

He is a little puzzled by the request, but is happy to offer his services, just the same.

"Worth knowing, thanks Al, and again, thanks for the meat."

Breakfast over, Lancelot seems a little lost as to just what is expected of him.

"Al, what to do suggest that I do this morning?" Asking, is clearly the most reasonable and obvious thing to do.

"Well sire, the horses haven't been out since we arrived. Might it not be an idea to take them out for a bit of exercise?" Al is finding living in this castle, even with the liberty and support of his childhood friends, rather oppressive.

Any excuse to be outside for a few hours would be most appreciated, and to take the horses for a run, that, that would be, a taste of paradise.

Now this was an idea that Lancelot can well see the sense of. He turns to the youth, smiles, lifts his index finger, and quotes; "make it so."

Al, who has no idea that Lancelot is quoting anything at all, still manages to fully understand the message and goes off to organise the preparation of the horses.

They have been riding for about a half hour. And had left all signs of civilisation behind them, almost ten minutes ago.

Lancelot needs to talk, Lancelot wants to talk, Lancelot is going to talk.

Al doesn't really know how can be so sure of this, but certain, he is.

 "Al, what I'm about to say is in strictest confidence." Whatever signs that he had picked up on, he wasn't wrong.

"Sire, I am your squire, I would never repeat anything that you might choose to confide in me." Don't block him now.

"Good, right."

The horses are starting to show signs of restlessness, they haven't the habit of living in boxes.

They both are aware of the reactions of their horses. Talking will have to wait, just a little longer, there is another, more pressing matter to deal with.

"Ready?", there is no need to be more explicit than that. Al gives a quick nod, and they loosen the reins. The horses read the signal, and they're off.

Al falls slightly back, the violence of his horse's gallop is slightly unexpected and leaves him a bit unprepared.

However, that magical unknown experience of horsemanship and the months of riding with Dena and Lancelot, save him from any mishap.

Soon, he is flowing with the pace, the top half of his body, still and calm, while his hips and waist follow the pounding rhythm of the galloping hooves.

Galloping, over open fields, on a clear summer's morning, is as close to the perfect dream, that anyone is likely to ever experience.

Ten minutes of this and the horses are starting to tire. Al's pony has little chance to keep up with the huge and heavy knight's stallion, but lightness and suppleness have made it that it was not left so very far behind.

Lancelot is relaxing, leaning on a fallen log, his horse happily grazing on the fresh, morning washed grass, when Al finally catches up.

"You'll do well to get a bigger horse, boy."

"Just as soon as you might desire to offer me one, sire."

The easy familiarity with the youth, as soon as they are out of the confines of the walled city, confirms Lancelot's sense of security, talking to the boy.

"Al, come sit here, beside me."

"As soon as I've seen to old Dobbin here, sire."

He smoothly unties the bridle and sends the horse off to graze.

"Would you care for some refreshment? I have ale and sweetcakes."

"Yes, yes that would be a good idea." Al digs out the snacks and hands them over to the knight. "Will you also not share some with me?"

The squire had dutifully brought his master the food and drink, but nothing for himself.

"I have also something for myself."

He has also brought some food and drink for himself, however, a squire can not be expected to take the same food from the kitchen for himself, as he takes for his knight.

"Then bring it out, I wish for company." Lancelot invites him to sit alongside him.

When they are eventually both settled, Lancelot lets some minutes pass, before starting the conversation.

"Al, things at the court are not as simple as I had hoped that they would be."

"Yes, sire," he responds, helpfully.

"Things, are, to be truthful, rather complicated."

"Would that be due to the queen still expressing feelings for you? The king wishing that you had never returned? Or to do with your feelings for the lady Angelique?"

Better get it all out on the open as quickly as possible, that will do away with his master having to painfully draw out his secrets.

Lancelot nearly spills the skin of ale all over his yellow riding breeches.

"What the?" He stops for several moments, at a loss for words.

"I, I do apologise, m'lord. I didn't think to speak out of turn. I just presumed that you wished to speak of such matters, and I thought to assist you. Please, please, please, your grace, I beg your mercy."

'By our Lady, I didn't think that he'd react like this. So, so, stupid.'

Lancelot is obviously shocked; but whether by his apologies, or by his clear knowledge and assessment of this complicated situation, Al is in no way able to guess,

"Shut up for a moment, will you. No, no it's all right, you didn't say anything wrong. I was just rather surprised that would know all that."

"Sire, the servers at the banquet are there to see to every wish and desire of the guests. They are particularly attentive to all that passes." He allows himself to breath normally again.

Your interactions with the royal family, have been closely observed by, at least, six pairs of attentive eyes." Better not to reveal that he has also been spying on him.

By now, almost every person working within the castle knows of your dilemma."

That he has been able to clarify and confirm during his late meal in the kitchen.

The famous knight, seems most preoccupied by his drink. The squire is starting, once again to be concerned that he has said too much.

Then, he hears the soft rumble, that grows, and grows, until Lancelot is shaking like an epileptic.

The body contorts in all directions, as the howl of laughter erupts, volcanically from his gut.

"And I was panicking that someone might have noticed something. Now there's nothing more to hide."

"But sire, it is only the castle servants that know. Nothing that happens in the castle is ever reported outside of our circle, it would be too dangerous, they could lose their lives."

He has to reassure him that there is no danger of his being found out.

"You, serious?"

"Surely. It is like that in any service. All the members of the staff know pretty much all the secrets of the household, but no one would ever think to tell."

"But what of the members of the family, wouldn't they get to hear?"

Al stops for a moment, clearly shocked at the idea.

"One of the staff, talking to their betters, telling them secrets about another member of the household? That could never happen, it just isn't done."

The older man, relaxes even more.

"So, the fact that all the staff know of my, how did you express it, yes, my dilemma, doesn't mean that anyone else is aware of it?"

"Only you sire, and you already knew." That's actually quite funny.

"And if I hadn't already known?"

"Then this conversation never happened."

"Quite right, it never happened."

"But, but how did they know about my feelings for the princess? I never said or did anything out of the ordinary, last night."

"Not last night."

"Not last night?"

"Why, when you first arrived in the courtyard. From the very moment that you first noticed her, you could hardly keep your eyes off of her."

"And you noticed that?" This, he is not ready to admit.

"No, that was someone much closer."

"And might I be bold enough to ask, who?"

The youth stops to decide, a good newspaperman never discloses his sources, but then again, he is but a humble squire.

"I don't suppose that it can do any harm to say. It was the maid Marion; she is Lady Angelique's lady in waiting."

"The one that give her the yellow ribbons to wear."

"That I wouldn't know, sire. Maybe it was just one of those coincidences of life."

That is also not for the knight to be made aware of, at least, not yet.

Whether Lancelot is one hundred percent sure of the veracity of his denial, is of little importance, as he decides to let it pass.

"Sire, the sun is approaching its zenith, it is time to return for dinner. Shall I prepare the horses?" Al feels that this moment of sharing is starting to become rather too uncomfortable for him, high time for them to be getting back.

"No, I'm quite capable to see to put Mel's bridle back on, you see to your half-pint, and I'll see to mine."

Although his jaw is set, and his voice, firm, his eyes twinkle.

Maybe knowing, that all the castle mice, are aware of the theatre piece, being played out, in front of the public, is somewhere, comforting.

Anyway, he seems much more relaxed on the return leg of their morning's ride.

Ch. 23 A Pleasant Walk, a Pleasant Talk

Lancelot enters his room and throws himself onto the bed.

"Oh God, oh God."

"Should I call again for the priest?" A voice appears from the shadows, just in advance of the young man who manifests himself, seconds later.

"Al! Do you always sleep here?"

"It's much more comfortable than where they have lodged me. And I'm closer at hand, if you should have need of me. How can I be of service?"

"I've just had the most unpleasant encounter, very unpleasant."

"Was it one of the servants?"

"No, it was one of the knights. He was this …"

"..If it please your grace, it might be more discrete to not talk about other members of the royal household, while in the castle."

Al is fully aware of likelihood of being overheard, he has, and likely will continue to use this useful source of information.

"What?"

"Sire, walls have ears."

"Even in here?"

"Would it not be a pleasant afternoon to go and take in the woods, and maybe practice some swordsmanship?" He seems to be having trouble integrating his squire's counsel.

"And why not?"

It took them a good half hour to prepare themselves and to find an appropriate clearing, in the woods.

Al would have carried all the equipment, had the knight not insisted. So each man carried, not only their own swords, but also the heavy, leather jerkin and gloves that are used when practicing.

He has not handled his sword since that fateful day in the forest, and is interested to see how well he will do, especially as he has no way to ascertain how much he was inspired due to the urgency of the situation.

Anyway, there is only one way to find out.

"Are you prepared, sire?"

It takes him a moment to get used to the tight leather protection, but as he is keen to start …

"Let's go to it."

Al salutes him, and Lancelot mirrors the action.

Both men, eye the other waiting to see what he will do, waiting for an opening, waiting for a strike.

Al attacks first, a simple cut towards the arm, the knight's sword, totally vertical, arcs smoothly round, the swords meet, a bell chimes.

The younger is now open and vulnerable, a diagonal slash down and across, seeking the open chest. But no, he is no longer there.

A dance step back, and he is out of danger's path. The blade swishes down, only to curve back, with a deft, flick of the wrist.

They are again defended and ready.

They circle, Lancelot thrusts, direct, testing. Simple parry, but it is just a feint, the knight spins the sword, up and round.

The action of a horizontal parry, leaves the whole of the right arm open and attackable.

The twisting sword, is targeted for the unprotected limb, but again, a turn and jump, and the prey, has flown the coop.

And so, to and fro, they go. Thrust and parry and dance.

Al is thrilled at his fencing skills, and would be happy to go on, but he hasn't forgotten that this was supposed to be a pretext to get out of the castle, so they could talk without being overheard.

"So this knight, what did he look like?"

"Quite big, heavy, solid. Dark hair; thick, but cut straight, just at level of the ears, thin, dark moustache, beady eyes, thin lips."

"Was he coming down from the west wing?"

"Yes, I believe that he was."

"That would be Sir Gawain."

"Well it certainly might, but he wasn't very civil with me."

"He cannot be happy that you have been reinstated into the household."

"Why, did I sleep with his wife, or daughter, or mother?"

"It is not a jesting matter." How could he not remember, even this?

"What isn't?"

"Gaheris and Gareth, were his younger brothers."

"And?"

"They both died by your hand."

"What? I killed two boys?"

"No, they were already men, other knights of the round table."

"Why would I kill them?"

"It is said that it was an accident, that in the smoke, you couldn't see who they were, and so, unfortunately, you killed them." He was in the crowd, he had seen all that could be seen.

"And Gawain, has never forgiven me?"

"Would you easily forgive someone that killed your brothers?" He shakes his head, how could he have forgotten even this?

"But surely, I must have tried to apologise."

"And would that bring them back to life?" Doesn't he realise that he is talking about having killed his brothers, not just spilled some mead on their favourite feast-gown.

"No, of course not. I seem to have more enemies at the court than friends."

"Naw, I judge that it's about equal. After all, you've two ladies, looking out for you."

"Please, don't talk about that now, I've no idea how I'm to advance my suite of Angelique, as long as the queen still has eyes for me."

Lancelot, clearly feels safe to share his relationship concerns with his squire, and then again, who else might he talk so openly with?

"Not to worry, I'm sure that everything will pan out. Shall we continue a little more?"

"Oh, am I going to whop you, this time?" And so they continue.

Ch. 24 Food for Thought

Lancelot walks into the dining room, the royal parents are arguing. It is not unheard of for them to argue. He is clearly uncomfortable, and hesitates to re-exit, when Alice, the serving wench enters and motions him to continue towards the table.

Al is once more secreted in his eyrie, he is still concerned for his master and the complicated situation that he has found himself in.

"You had no right." The king is not in the best of moods. They have not yet noticed that he has entered.

"I had every right in the world."

"You should have waited to ask me."

"Waited for you to sober up?"

"I wasn't drinking; I was in a meeting."

"You still reek of whiskey."

"I can choose to have a drink of Irish Whiskey, if I wish."

"Anyway, it's done now."

"Well it can be undone."

"You don't think that you are going to humiliate me in front of everybody?"

"You shouldn't have agreed."

"You should have been here, we have guests."

"No we don't, …" Lancelot steps out of the shadows.

"Good evening."

"Ah. Lancelot, just the man I need."

'Just the last man you need, if he wouldn't have noticed him,' the squire smiles a wry smile to himself.

"Your highness?"

"Duke Erik, I don't trust him."

"Yes, your majesty?" The knight is perplexed.

"Your squire, he looks an intelligent boy."

'By our lady, what does he want with me now?"

"Al is a very resourceful young man."

'Thank you, sire. I will not forget your kindness.'

"Could you spare him for a day or two?"

"As you wish, m'lord."

"I want him to keep an eye on Duke Erik, and to report directly to me."

'Spy? Well, that might be more interesting than what I'm filling my time with.'

"Arthur, he will do no such thing."

'Yes I will, yes I will. Please, please someone say something.'

"Fine, then he will saddle his mule, and be off, first thing tomorrow morning."

'Well played Your Majesty.'

"You wouldn't dare."

'Oh yes he would.'

"Just try me, m'lady, just try me."

Knowing the King Arthur, Al well knows full well what the old fox was capable of. And it seemed that the Queen Guinevere does too.

"Fine, but he will report to both of us."

'Coup de Grace, well played, Your Majesty.'

"Fine."

"Fine."

Arthur, he knew, could turn incredibly warm and friendly at any given moment, and this was such a moment.

"So, tell us of some of your exploits, it's been so very long since we've had the pleasure to hear of your adventures."

'Oops, that could be a little difficult. This is really not the moment to ask him to brag about his achievements, since, I'm sure that he has no idea, at all, of that which he is supposed to have done.

He couldn't even remember his own name. So, sire, how are you going to waggle out of this?'

Lancelot stops for a long moment, then, smiling, vaguely in Al's direction.

"Sire, if I might make as so bold, if it would it please your majesty, I will call for my squire to come a recount my undertakings. That way he can already have some contact with the Duke and begin his mission. "

'Does he know that I am here? That could be embarrassing.'

"You see husband; how modest he is? He cannot allow himself to boast of his accomplishments, he needs ask another, for that service."

"Alice! Send someone to find Lancelot's squire."

It is then that he realises exactly what his master has set him up for, and that he needs to get back to their chamber before others notice his absence.

"His name is Al," is the last thing that he hears before scarpering out and back up the stairs.

He arrives a few moments before Alice, and disappears into his sleeping corner.

"Al, are you here?"

"Who is it? He continues his charade.

"You know full well that it is me, Alice. Don't be playing the fool, we know that you've been keepin' an eye on Lancelot, and we all knows full why."

"Just tryin' not to be too obvious."

"Trust us, we are all your friends."

"Thanks, I really need my friends now."

"So, are you ready for your recital?"

"N', n', n', no."

"You can do this. I'll come for you after they've finished the main course. That way they'll be relaxed, the king will be drunk, and all will be well."

"Thanks, I'll do the best that I can." And so she leaves, and he gets to work trying to remember all the words to the The Ballad of the White Knight.

Panicking to not remember all of it, he descends back to the downstairs and enters the kitchen.

Only to find that the entire kitchen staff, singing loud and off key, the very same piece.

"Come Al, come sing with us, it'll help if you sing it a few times full before you go before the king."

He is a little surprised that Hélène, the all powerful and dreadful dragon of the fiery kitchen hearths, would put her cooking staff at his disposal to help him overcome his stage-fright.

Al smiles at the sweaty group in deep appreciation, and they all restart to sing.

They manage to go through the ballad several times before Alice comes in to find him.

The diners are just about to begin the dessert when there is a sound from just behind the door.

"Who is skulking there?"

" 'Tis, I, m'm'lady, I was summoned, by his highness." 'Okay, now it's show-time.'

"Then come in then, m'boy." Arthur is in good spirits this evening, more than likely in both senses.

Al comes in, a little sheepishly, he has little direct experience of contact with the royal household.

"We were told that you will recount the exploits of your knight."

"Here, in front of everyone?" He looks at Lancelot, in alarm, hoping to be saved from this awful situation."

He somehow hadn't counted on the Lady Angelique being there, not that he realises in the moment that it is because of her presence that he has suddenly panicked.

"I'm sorry, but I find that I cannot recite my own adventures, so I thought that you might do that service for me."

"Well, young man, can you, or can't you?" The attitude is as direct as usual.

"I, I, I will do my best, your majesty." "'I don't have any other choice.'

Al walks to the front of the table, and turns to face his audience.

"The, the Ballad of the White Knight," he takes a gulp of air, closes his eyes, willing himself to believe that he is still in the kitchen, singing amongst friends, and so, begins.

"And I will tell, a glorious tale,"
Of strength, of courage and valour.
Of how a man became a knight
Of good and Godly power

The white knight came,
And the white knight stood
The white knight fought
For God and good."

He can feel that it is going well. Without noticing, he has opened his eyes and has scanned the reaction of the nobles, for which he is singing.

His first glance is towards Lancelot, to gage how a friendly critic is appreciating his efforts.

The knight is gently smiling and tapping his fingers in time with the beat.

Already greatly relieved, he then dares to survey the others.

Arthur is also smiling, but his gaze is already glassy, so it is difficult no know if it is his efforts or the effect of the alcohol,

The queen seems quietly amused.

The Duke Erik is clearly enjoying the entertainment.

And finally, the Lady Angelique?

Finally, he dares to look in her direction. She captures his regard and gently gives a slight nod of the head. A clear nod of approval.

However, he cannot but also notice just how close she and the Lord Erik are leaning together, maybe the rumours are true, after all.

Al takes a deep breath and launches into the rest of the song.

"The son of Ban, and belle Elaine,
Lost their lands to Claudas
Was stolen by a water sprite
Who hid him 'neath the surface.

And so he grew, both proud and strong
These gifts were there to take
In her realm of magic lore
The Lady of the Lake

The white knight came,
And the white knight stood
The white knight fought
For God and good

And then he came to Arthur's court
To Arthur's court he came,
And 'twas taken to be knight
On behest of just Gawain

Hooded men, they stole the queen
By northern Pul they took her
'Til Lancelot the bold and brave,
To the King, returned her

The white knight came,
And the white knight stood
The white knight fought
For God and good

The Dolorous Guard,
And the Copper Knight
He must slay ten and ten
But when he reached
The second wall
The knight had gone again.

Then more knights
They do appear
For my Lord to take
But help will come
This magic day,
The Lady of the Lake.

They lead him to
An old graveyard
There rests a metal block
To be raised
By the pure of heart
'Tis true a magic rock.

For written clear
Beneath the stone
The name, wrote on that spot,
He lifts it up
The crowds they cheer,
The name is Lancelot.

The white knight came,
And the white knight stood
The white knight fought a lot
Now for our king,
And God and good
All praise Sir Lancelot."

In fact, he is very good. And his audience is most
appreciative.

"Bravo, bravo, well done. Alice, bring our young bard a
chair and a glass of sweet wine." The king is clearly
pleased with the recital.

Or maybe not.

Al knows the working of the court, and of this king, if
anything, a little too well.

It is not usual to invite a squire or even a bard, to sit before his king, even less so to offer him expensive, sweet wine. No, there is likely to be something else behind.

Of course, the spying on Erik, Arthur is making sure of Al's loyalty, by overpraising him for the poem.

The meal now over, the hosts and guests make ready to retire.

"Lancelot, you and your squire, I will speak with you a moment, come up to my chambers."

Al starts to panic and looks to his knight, but Lancelot smiles and nods reassuringly to the unhappy youth.

"You know the Duke Erik?" Once in his chambers, Arthur wastes no time opening up the conversation."

"Ay, m'lord." Of course he does; Erik has been a frequent visitor to the castle for many years, and his relationship with Lady Angelique had been open to much speculation by all and sundry.

"You know that his father is planning to attack Camelot?"

"So I have heard." Of course he has heard, wasn't he the one to have intercepted the ransom note addressed to Galahaut, himself?

"Do you not believe it so?" Al panics again, and looks towards Lancelot for support.

"We have seen no signs of any army, sire." Why now would he suddenly defend his old friend, after believing the threat, so much so that he helped to steal the sceptre?

"That is because it is a secret army, one doesn't see a secret army, or it wouldn't be secret army, would it not?" The king is more than sure of his position.

"No m'lord. It wouldn't be a secret army if we had seen it. My squire, who has not had the opportunity to be clearly informed about the presence of a secret army, has been ignorant of its existence."

'What's he talking about, I'm the one that showed him the letter?'

"Yes, I suppose that I can understand that."

'After a skin full of whiskey, I doubt that he can understand much of anything.'

"Well, there is a secret army, and they are planning a surprise attack on Camelot. I think that Erik has come here to spy on us and look for our weaknesses."

Al, for want of anything better to do, is standing nodding his head.

"So, I would like you, in a discrete manner, to sort of, keep an eye on him."

'I'd better act surprised, or he'll guess that I've been spying on him.'

"You mean that you want me to spy on him?" Al is being rather direct.

"Exactly," The king seems quite happy to call a spade, a spade.

"So, is that all clear?" Again, Al looks to his knight for confirmation.

"If his majesty requests this little service from you, then it is our duty and our pleasure to fulfil this task to the very best of our abilities."

"To the very best of my abilities," it is easier to repeat the knight, than think of anything different to respond.

"Good, excellent. I shall send for you from time to time. And, you are released from all your other duties, towards your knight. However, you will still need to look after him, a little, or people will notice.

So, is that all clear?"

'Do you think that I'm a total idiot? Maybe if you drank a little less, you'd realise that there's something fishy going on here.'

Al doesn't realise where his unusually disrespectful attitude is coming from, but the stress of the evening is starting to tell on him.

"Yes, yes, your majesty." Al is stuttering again, but still is a particularly stressful situation.

"Good, excellent. Well? What are you both waiting for? I've still masses of things to do, tonight."

The two visitors, bow and leave.

They head back to their bedroom, exhausted, but both feeling rather satisfied with the outcome of this evening's events.

Ch. 25 Of Birds, Breakfast and Bards

Al did not sleep well this night and is irritated by the chirping of birds, awake bright and early.

He is angry, he is jealous, he is confused.

Yes, he has been aware of Angelique most of all his life.

Being several years older than him, she was already old enough to be riding through the city, at the time that he was allowed out alone.

And yes, she was, she is pretty. And yes, as a young adolescent he had sexually fantasised about her.

Surely, he had also fantasised over Marion and half a dozen different girls, some older, some, the same age, some younger.

And, he, like most of the townsfolk knew of the closeness of Erik and Angelique, and as they were both well-liked and respected, most people were more than happy to dream that they would, someday, 'tie the knot'.

And yet, for some inexplicable reason, since seeing her, in the memory of Lancelot, his feelings towards her had changed.

For now, what he is feeling is anger, anger and jealousy.

He is jealous that she has feelings for Erik.

Could it be due to the young Lord's attitude towards him while they were lodged with King Galahaut? True, he had had no interactions with him, quite ignored him, while most of the other members of the royal family treated him with some care.

Yes, he could have felt slighted by him, but could it explain this jealousy and anger?

Round and round, it turns round in his young head, like a spinning weather cock, during a tempest.

'He's not going to have her. Lancelot is love with her. He is my master, and I'm going to make sure that it is to him that she will turn her attentions.'

There, he has found a solution, now there is just the small matter of having her fall in love with him, that, and getting the royal couple to accept him as their future son-in-law.

Although, if he had stopped to think on it, he might have thought to imagine another, more reasonable project, but, in that moment, it seems totally obvious.

And so, smiling to himself, he gets up quietly, so not to awaken, his, still sleeping master.

The very same master, that Al has now decided to introduce as the future prince of Camelot.

He goes downstairs to procure himself something to eat.

Hélène, the kitchen queen, is busy scolding one of the helpers. It seems that some of the vegetables that she had asked for, are not up to her expectations.

Al reflects that she must have a room next to the kitchens, as she always seems to be here.

"And what would our famous troubadour desire for breakfast?"

Al, who has always been more than a little overawed by this massive, energetic woman, is having a difficult time integrating the idea that she is going out of her way to be nice to him.

Although, he is not at all surprised to find that one of the usual morning dishes, a form of meat broth, is simmering over the fireplace.

What does surprise him greatly, is that he is being served a portion.

"But this is only for the knights and the royal household."

He is even a little scared of what might happen if he is found out to have eaten food that is considered, 'above his station'.

"That's me own choice, I am needin' for you to taste it for me, to see if it's good enough for the 'igh table." She smiles a gappy smile, and hands him the bowl.

"Héléne," he decides he can risk calling her by her first name.

"Yes?"

He shares with her his project.

"I want to get Lady Angelique to fall in love with Sir Lancelot."

She stops for a moment, before replying.

"You ain't joshin' with me?"

"You know that he's in love her?"

"But she's eyes are fer young Erik, 'as been, since f'ever."

"I don't think that the king is in a mind to favour such an alliance."

"Hush, don't you be talkin' abart that. Loose tongues ends up on the floor."

This is a real threat, Al has known more than one unfortunate soul that has lost his ability to talk, after forgetting to hold his tongue.

"Eat your broth and use your mouth for what it does best."

"Got it, eating."

"No, making up stuff."

And with that obscure reflection, she turns and heads back towards the unfortunate helper, who is about to merit, yet a second helping of tongue lashing.

'Making up stuff, making up stuff,' he mulls over her words as he enjoys the hot, meaty dish.

'Yes, yes, of course.' "Thanks Hélène," he calls out cheerfully as he rushes out of the kitchens.
He needs some stuff from Lancelot's chamber, but he doesn't want him to know what he is up to.

Quietly he slides open the door. It wouldn't be a disaster if the knight is still there, but it would frustrate his plans for a while.

However, the room is empty. He cannot risk being seen, so he steals the parchment, ink and quill and secretes himself in an unused horsebox where to advance his plan.

After returning the ink and quill to their room, it is now time to hunt out his master.

Not having any other idea of where he might be at this time, Al makes his way to the dining room.

As there might well be any member of the royal household taking breakfast, he enters discretely into the room.

Still concealed within the small entrance lobby, he can make out Lancelot sitting at the breakfast table, deep in conversation with Friar Brendan. The holy man is eating and talking at the same instant.

"… So, things are turning more to your liking?"

"Things are not too bad, Arthur, has decided that I might be useful, in some complicated affair that he is cooking up, so he has decided to be nice with me.

Then, the good Lady Guinevere, is being reasonable, but I still don't know how to get her to release her desire towards me, and not be jealous of any relationship that I might succeed to build with Angelique."

"And of the fair princess?"

"Well, Angelique seems more open to notice that I exist. Although, I'm a little worried about the good Duke Erik, she seems to have a very close relationship with him."

"I would doubt, that, in the present circumstances, Arthur, would be generally open to such an alliance."

"Yes, there, I must agree with you. I think that, for some reason of his own, he is particularly keen to wage this war against Galahaut."

"So you don't believe that he is amassing a secret army to invade Camelot?"

Al decides that it is high time that he made his presence known. He wouldn't want anyone to think that he was intending to eavesdrop, even if that just might be the truth.

"I really don't know what to believe. Al, is something wrong?" The young man has entered, looking rather out of breath.

"No, m'lord," he smiles, "I was just in haste to find you. Good morning, father."

The panting was proven to be a good idea

" 'Morning, my son."

"What has happened?"

"It is just a little matter, that you might wish to take care of."

"What sort of matter?"

"Of the heart."

"I'm not understanding you." If anything, Lancelot is starting to get irritated by the opaque discourse of his squire.

"Could you be a little more clear?"

"Walls, ears."

"I think that he wishes for you to go with him, somewhere a little more private. Thank you for your pleasant company over breakfast, it has been most agreeable. Good morning."

It is clear that the spiritual guide thinks that he should follow the boy, so he finishes off his ale, picks up a sweet bread and throws it at his protégé.

"Here, you've more than likely not eaten properly, it's rather good."

It is, more than likely, the best that he could think of as an immediate form of apology for telling him off. For he surely is thinking of something in the knight's best interests.

They arrive several minutes later in Lancelot's quarters. There is some sort of writing desk set up, with ink, quill and several pages of virgin parchment invitingly placed on it."

"What is all this for?"

"To write with?"

"You want that I take back your breakfast?"

"I have been to the tavern…"

"So that's where you've been, is it?"

"To meet with a bard who I know."

"A bard? A singer?"

"And a poet."

"And why would you be meeting with a poet."

"For this." He pulls out a folded object from within his jerkin, which he hands directly over to his knight.

Better than to ask what it is, Lancelot opens the document and starts to read, stops, sits down on the bed, and continues to peruse its contents.

"It's good, really nice. Who's it for?"

"The Lady Angelique."

"I don't …" then his gaze falls on the writing equipment. "Am I to recopy this?"

"And I will see that it appears in her boudoir."

"And she will know that it comes from me?"

"It might be easier to guess, if you signed it, something like 'Your newest admirer' ".

"So, I have work to do."

Ch. 26 Crime and Punishment

The day had been unremarkable, at least for the conquering hero. They have ridden in the morning, and fenced in the afternoon.

Dinner had been a subdued affair; Erik was waiting to meet with Arthur, Al waited on his knight.

It is clear that everyone is secretly of the opinion that it would bring no benefit, as the King seems rigid in his position, even if all the company wished for it to be otherwise.

And so they came to supper. Al, who is not expected to be there, spent some minutes spying on them, but quickly became bored. And as he hadn't eaten yet, made his way down to the kitchens, to see what he could scrape up.

He was just finishing up some sops when Alice appears, she is looking for him.

"The princess has sent me to get you."

"What 'ave you dun now?" Hélène sounds concerned.

"D'd'd'don't know." His heart has started to play a military tattoo.

"Don't keep 'er waiting then."

He takes heed of her advice and rushes up the stairs and into the dining room.

"M'lady, you sent for me?"

'Are they looking at me, as if I'm guilty of something?'

"Yes, we were pleased with your rendition of last eve, and wish to benefit from your availability to brighten this one, equally." The young mistress of the house is smiling at him.

Only, he feels that he shouldn't be totally trusting this smile. A phrase enters into his head, 'never smile at a crocodile'. Although he has absolutely no idea where it has come from, or what, in this context, it might mean.

"But I have no more to relate of the exploits of my master." He would very much like to be excused and return to finish his supper.

"That is of no matter, as I have the material that I wish for you to perform. I trust that you are capable to read." The Lady Angelique continues on her quest.

"And to write, I was educated by the clergy."

"Excellent. Ah, Marion, good, give it to the boy."

Marion, who has just entered, brings a scroll of parchment to Al, it looks rather familiar, she does not look him in the eye.

"We have just had the good fortune to come across this work, and I think that it would be amusing to share it."

He opens up the scroll, and by reflex, looks directly at Lancelot. The knight discreetly shrugs his shoulders, there is nothing that he can do, so, he does, nothing.

"Please," she smiles sweetly at the uncomfortable youth, "you recited so well."

He coughs slightly to clear his throat, takes several deep breaths, and begins to read.

"The Dream

In my youth, I had a dream,
And in that in the dream,
I floated high.
Dancing meadows
Singing brooks
All of these,
They passed me by."

He stops, and looks up, as waiting for something.

"Is there more?" It is the first time that the queen has spoken in a while.

"Yes, I believe that there is. Why do you stop?" The princess presses him on.

"It is a love poem, m'lady."

"And so do I believe."

"It is quite an intimate thing." The young man is clearly fighting an invisible battle, that maybe only Lancelot is really clear about.

"Please continue." Again, he looks over for support, but there really is nothing that can be done.

"In my youth, I had a dream,
And in that in the dream,
A form
Standing lonely
By the shores
All alone
Forsworn.

In my youth, I had a dream,
And in that in the dream,
A child
Hardly bigger
Then a sheep
Abandoned sure
And wild.

In my youth, I had a dream,
And in that in the dream,
I, to her side
She never moved
Nor made a sound
But gave a start
To run and hide.

In my youth, I had a dream,
And in that in the dream,
I bent my knee
I showed my hands
Were open wide
I'd always
Leave her free.

In my youth, I had a dream,
And in that in the dream,
I gave my heart
To this innocent
To this pure
Knowing
I must part."

Again, he stops, he is desperate, he starts to sweat. He
looks first to Lancelot, then to Angelique, and even,
finally, to the queen. He must know that he will need to
read it to the end, but it is paying a heavy toll for doing
so.

"In my youth, I had a dream,
And in that in the dream,

Was time to go
I cut her image
Into my soul
Where the seed
Might grow.

In my youth, I had a dream,
Which haunts me all my life
She was the angel that I sought
Who must be my wife.

In my youth, I had a dream,
That no queen could pair
There is no love to offer me
My heart, it isn't there.

In my youth, I had a dream,
You must remember sure
For you were also there, my dear
Standing by the shore.

In my youth, I had a dream,
But now that dream has passed
I live here, in this now
Nothing more is asked

In my youth, I had a dream,
And now that dream's come true
You are all my waking dreams
All my dreams are you."

And so he stops, empty, drained, ashamed.

"Is there something wrong, I thought that it was quite charming. Angelique, where did you come across such a gem?" A motherly interest?

"It was livered to me, only today."

"To you, and who was it from?"

"A secret admirer."

"How amusing. A secret admirer, that is also a poet."

" 'Fraid not. For you see, the poet stands before us."

Angelique is looking straight at him, there can be no mistake.

"Who …?" But it is more than obvious. Just to look at the appalling discomfort that the boy is showing, is proof enough.

"You would have done better than to try and hide in the old stables, when you were scratching your old, dried skin. You were seen by my groom, as he went to fetch my horse, early this morning."

No one speaks for a moment. He looks over to Marion. At least it wasn't her that betrayed him.

"Well, I for one think that it is a very beautiful poem," he turns to the Duke, in appreciation of that support.

"And I'm sure that there were very good reasons for his doing it," the queen turns, and to his very great surprise, smiles at Lancelot. "Erik, do you have any gold on you?"

"Aye, m'lady."

"Give the boy a noble, a noble coin, for a noble poem. … Now off you go, I'm sure that you have not yet had time to finish your supper." And with that, he is officially excused.

As he is rushing to leave, he cannot but look to see the reaction of the recipient of the poem.

"There is no shame in an admirer seeking out another to craft his feelings in beautiful words. It is a time-honoured tradition, and you should think yourself very fortunate to have such a thoughtful suitor."

Angelique is clearly totally nonplussed by the queen's reaction. And as she doesn't seem to be able to think of anything appropriate to say, she wishes everyone a good evening, and exits behind him.

Al hesitates whether to go back down to the kitchen, but he has since lost all interest in finishing off his meal.

Someone else is leaving the dining room, it is Lancelot.

Discretely he follows the troubled hero back up to their room. He can hear him muttering to himself.

"Is there nothing that is as it seems?" As he shakes his head in despair, climbing the hard, stone steps, up to his safe, soft bed.

The young squire takes a moment to smile to himself, this has been a particularly successful day, after all.

Ch. 27 A Pleasant Walk, a Pleasant Talk, Along the Briny Beach

Of course it isn't a real beach, and there certainly are no oysters.

Al is walking along the river Shaw, the name, he was led to believe was something to do with it passing through a small wood.

He is meant to be meeting Lancelot somewhere here, but, as yet, he is still alone.

The space gives him time to reflect on his adventures of yesterday.

Hélène's suggestion had not taken long to land and for him to come up with his plan to write a poem and make it seem that it was from the knight.

It was only when he was safely, (or so he believed at the time), secreted in the horse box, that he realised exactly the enormity of the challenge.

And so he did, what he would always do when faced with something that he didn't know how to do, he fell asleep. After all, he had slept little the preceding night.

And in that sleep, he dreamed a dream. And that very dream became the basis of his poem.

However, it still wasn't so easy as all that. For not only had he the challenge of writing the poem, he also had to deal with the totally unexpected emotional upheaval that it awoke in him.

There he was, sitting on the old straw of the box, rough wooden slats on all sides, and still the strong smell of horse, underneath and all round him.

'Can't do this. I cannot write this. I cannot be feeling, what it is that I'm feeling.' And yet he must, and yet he did.

Then he pocketed the parchment, ink and quill and returned to his and the knight's chamber. Replacing the pen and ink, he thought to hide the scroll somewhere in the room, but then decided that the safest bet would be to keep it on his person.

From there he went in search of Lancelot and brought him back upstairs to copy the love letter in his own hand.

That done, it was only necessary to convince
Marion to check if the coast was clear, steal into
Angelique's chambers and leave it on her dressing
table.

At that time, he had imagined that his labours for
the day had ended, only, they hadn't.

He had stolen into the kitchens to grab himself some
lunch, when his little adoptive brother, now calling
himself Alexander, appeared.

"You have been summoned by the king. Come
now." As the ruler's emissary, he had given himself
full rights to boss his older brother about. Not that
he hadn't been doing that most of both of their lives,
but now, with an even greater air of authority.

Al gulped down a last mouthful of sweet mead,
wiped his mouth with the back of his hand, and
hurried on after his younger and shorter sibling.

They waited respectfully until their liege lord bade
them enter.

Alexander has clearly been enjoying his 'one-up'
position towards Al, however that was not to
continue.

It was only with the upmost of self-control that he
didn't stop to complain when the king ordered him
out, as he had important and secret business with
the squire.

Al reported faithfully all that he had observed that
the young duke had been doing. He gave special
emphasis to the time that Erik had been spending
with Angelique.

The king did not even try to hide his irritation of
this obvious complicity between his daughter and
the son of his declared enemy.

"Your grace?"

"Yes? Is there more?" He sounded tired,
exasperated.

Al looked hard at the polished wooden floor.

"Well, what is it?" His tone rose, danger signals
were sounding

"S',s',sire, I, I, I have something t't't'to say."

The sovereign realised that the boy has something
important that he wants to say, but is clearly much
too scared to express it.

Having benefitted from the squire's efforts on his
behalf, he took an emotional step back.

Then he calmed himself, and in a switch that only certain people are capable of, spoke in a particularly quiet and soothing voice.

"It's okay, please say to me what's on your mind. Don't have any fear, I trust that what you have to say can only be you trying to help."

His tone was clearly what was needed, as Al dared to look up to the king, and to begin speaking.

"S'sire, I, I think that I might have a s's'solution for several of your problems."

"You do, do you?" His voice remained soft, more inquisitive than aggressive.

"The friendliness between her majesty and the duke is not to your pleasure."

"Go on."

"And, and …," he faltered again.

"Speak, speak."

"It is said that her majesty, the queen is not totally uninterested in the attentions of my master …" He trailed off, waiting and fearing the explosion that expected to follow.

However, none came.

"And what would you suggest, young man?" He has still managed to keep his emotions under total control, the royal countenance remained neutral.

"You know that Sir Lancelot is smitten by her ladyship. If you were to give your support and approval to such a union, then, 'one stone, two birds'."

There is long silence, Al again feared that he had gone too far, but then, without further warning, the king gave out the mightiest roar of laughter.

"You are a wily one, I can see why Lancelot chose you for his squire. Fine, I will consent to his suit, to woo the Lady Angelique."

Al doesn't respond, he doesn't even move. The monarch noticed that there was something still not totally regulated.

"There's more?"

He took a deep before responding, "there's still Lady Guinevere, she must also agree."

"And you have some ideas on this?"

"The queen wishes that my master might continue to be welcome in your court.

If you suggest that by allying himself to the princess, he will become a permanent part of your court.

Otherwise, you are beginning to tire of his presence and have been thinking that his services have ceased to be of use to you, and that it might be time that he was on his way …"

Again, the end of the phrase tailed off, but this time, it has only been to leave a dramatic anti-climax.

The smile of the sly fox is true but dangerous, and Al has had the opportunity to experience it at the closest of proximities.

"I will take your thoughts into the closest of considerations. I thank you young man, here," he hunted around for a purse and draw a handful of coins which he gave to the relieved youth.

"Just one last thing."

"If you repeat just one word of what was spoken of today, it'll be the last word that ever passes your lips."

"I know how to hold my own counsel, your highness."

He nodded, smiled and threw him out of his chambers.

Al smiles at the memory, yes, it was a most successful day.

He finds the knight siting on a large boulder, amusing himself throwing small stones into the flowing waters.

"Something to eat or drink, m'lord?"

"Sure, why not?"

"Some bread 'n cheese, and a skin of ale?"

Lancelot allows the boy to feed and water him, before starting any real conversation. This is the first time that they have had any chance to talk since the evening.

Again, his squire, has been noticeable by his absence.

"Well?"

"Sire?"

"When were you going to tell me?"

"Tell you?"

"That it was you that wrote the poem?"

"Err, never. I hadn't planned to tell you."

"Why, the secret?"

There is a long pause, the younger man busies himself with looking for, and finding another skin. Lancelot waits patiently for his man to respond.

"I, I, I was ashamed."

"Of?"

His need is so great to share what he experienced, that the inappropriateness of who he is telling it to, has not the slightest effect to stop him.

"When I thought to write a poem for you, for her. I didn't realise that I also was having feelings for her.

I know that it is wrong, and I do so want to help you to get her, but when I was writing, I was feeling that I was in love with her.

I just felt so bad after, that I thought to lie to you, and said that a bard had written it."

"You are my most trusted companion, and, you will make a great writer and poet, one day. To be able to write a love poem for someone, to do it correctly, you need to be able to fall in love with them. And you did, and it was wonderful."

Al is happy enough to accept the knight's point of view, at least in this moment.

"You thought that it was acceptable?"

"It was really good, even Queen Guinevere liked it."

"She gave me a noble."

"And now, you are not only talented, you're also rich."

"Ay, m'lord."

"But where do you keep disappearing of to?"

"But you know, I'm a spy. I'm to keep my eyes on the Duke, and to report back to their majesties, as to his activities."

"And have you reported back, anything of interest?"

"Only a long walk in the gardens, with the princess."

"Oh."

"But not to worry."

"Why not?"

"Both the King and the Queen have forbidden her to be alone with him, from here on."

"Both of them?"

"Both."

"Then everything's fine."

"As you say, m'lord."

Lancelot is too pleased to notice the slight reticence in the squires reply, things seem to be definitely, on the up."

Ch. 28. Another Glass of Ale.

Arthur had chosen to join them for dinner, and not only that, is in rather an expensive mood.

He has filled the space with stories of his conquests, trials and tribulations.

Al has acquired some meat, bread and a large jug of ale. He is not sure what is likely to come to pass during this meal, but he has no intention to miss out on any of the drama.

Well ensconced in his comfy hide-a-way, he is ready for a pleasant and entertaining evening. After all, hasn't he earned it?

 "Have another glass of ale," Arthur invites the company, for the third or fourth time, all the while, topping up his own goblet, with, most likely, Irish Whiskey.

Then, quite suddenly, without any warning, the King turns to the White Knight, and addresses him in a confidential like manner.

"You know, if I was chasing after a particularly fine catch, I wouldn't let my squire, take his bow, and shoot at my quarry." And then makes a sort of theatrical wink.

It takes Lancelot a few seconds to catch on to exactly what the older man is referring to.

Al watches as the knight takes the time to ingest, that not only does King Arthur know of the story of the poem, but considers him, Lancelot as a suitable suiter for his daughter.

"I will surely confiscate both his bow and all his arrows," he finally responds.

"Maybe also his sword and knife," it seems that the Queen also wishes to establish that she is in on the game.

Lancelot, then turns to Angelique, "what sayeth you, m'lady?"

"Sharp objects, in the wrong hands, can cause much suffering."

'Strike one, strike two, strike three. No, more, hit one, hit two, hit three.' He feels as if his ale has been miraculously transformed into Arthur's whiskey. He starts to feel giddy, groggy but also gay.

"Then I musts need go and practice my skills."
Lancelot goes to get to his feet.

"A moment, before you leave us," Erik had hardly
spoken throughout the meal. "I feel that my
continued presence in Camelot will serve no more
useful purpose.

Hence, I will return and seek out my father, and
implore him to take me into his confidence about
his majesty's allegations.

If he denies them, I will insist that we return here
together, to confront Arthur with his false
accusations.

If he admits to them, I shall leave his court, I shall
return to Sorelais, and remain a neutral observer,
neither attacking nor supporting either party."

And with this, he rises from the table, bows to the
three nobles and salutes the knight.

Several moments pass in silence, there seems to be
nothing more to say. Lancelot also rises from his
seat, bows to each in turn, and takes his leave.

As there is little likelihood of any further fun, Al takes
the remains of his supper and returns to join the other
servants, and finish his meal with his friends in the
kitchen.

Ch. 29. Round and Round the Garden, Like a Teddy Bear

Lancelot is clearly troubled, he has dragged Al out, straight after lunch and they have been seeking Friar Brendan ever since.

He finally finds him in one of the castle gardens, contemplating a very beautiful rose bush. Or at least, he would have been if his eyes were still open, and there wasn't a gentle and rhythmic humming sound emitting from somewhere within his more than ample frame.

The squire hangs back and keeps a respectable distance, but not so much that he cannot clearly hear all that is being said.

"Wake up, I need to talk to you."

The sleeping friar jumps, opens his eyes, closes them and then repeats the action several times more. As if to confirm that the reality in which he now finds himself is indeed a reality, even more real than reality of the dream that he had just been having.

"Oh," finally, "it's you. Have you come to be
blessed, or to complain about something again?" he
adds defensively.

"No, I'm not here to complain, I'm quite happy with
the way that things are working out, I just need to
understand why you did it."

"Why I did what?"

"Organised with Arthur, Guinevere and Angelique,
that I shall marry her."

"Marry, who?" He doesn't seem to be totally awake
yet.

"Why Angelique of course."

"Of course," the priest, happily concurred.

"So why did you do it?"

"Do what?"

"Are you still asleep or are you drugged or
something? Why have you arranged for them to be
okay with me marrying Angelique?"

"But I didn't."

"What do you mean, you didn't?"

"Quite simple, really, I did nothing to interfere with the course of events."

"You mean that you've done nothing?"

"Nothing what-so-ever, I've told you several times, my only influence in these experiences is my ability to reflect with you on what is happening."

"So, you've done nothing to make it okay for me to marry Angelique?"

"The proof is complete, if only I've stated it thrice. No, I have done nothing to influence anyone to do anything.

Now, what do you think of these wonderful roses?"

Lancelot obviously thinks nothing of the roses.

He must surely still be wondering of which celestial agency could possibly have intervened to have created this unimaginable miracle.

Feeling that he would find it impossible to keep his promise to the king, if asked a direct question about any involvement that he might have in this story, he chooses caution, and melts out of sight.

He watches as Lancelot, fruitlessly searches for him.

Until, with nothing better to do, and no news about
the activities or where-a-bouts of his squire. He
calls for one of the stable boys to prepare his horse
and sets off for a long hard ride.

Ch. 30. Of Rose Marble and Gold

"Well at least he's left, and I can get back to my usual life."

Al is in the kitchen, finishing a snack of left-over sweet balls.

"But he hasn't left yet."

"What?" Marion is shocked by his unusually strong reaction.

"No, he, he'll be leaving later. What's the problem?"

"Marion, is he planning to meet the Lady Angelique before he goes?"

He is concerned that somehow all his manoeuvres to get Angelique and Lancelot together could be wrecked by some last-minute intervention of Erik's.

Marion hesitates a long moment before answering, there must be some ugly conflict of loyalty issues working themselves out, inside her pretty little head.

She takes a slow, long drink from the small tanker in her hand.

Then, watching intently, as she lowers the vessel onto the table, she whispers in a low tone.

"They are to meet in her chambers shortly. If you wish to discover what they wish to exchange, you would do well to hurry."

She then, carefully collects her plate and cup, takes them to washing area, cleans them, and returns to Al.

"I am going for a walk in the gardens, m'lady can find me there, if she needs me."

Picking up on her information, he clears his plates and hurries, as unobtrusively as possible, up to her lady's chambers.

The rooms have been fashioned with several fairly deep recesses build into the walls. On to one of these; rails, shelves and doors have been added to create a massive wardrobe.

By leaving one of doors slightly ajar, it is possible to see some parts of the room, but more importantly, one can easily hear what is being said.

He does not have to wait long before the princess enters.

She throws off her cloak and her boots, before
dropping heavily onto her ample, four poster bed.

Although he cannot see her from his vantage point,
he cannot hear any movement, and imagines that
she is trying to relax while waiting for Erik to
arrive.

There is a soft, tap, tap on her door.

She launches herself off of the bed, and hurries to
welcome him in.

The door opens and is then quietly closed.

There is a long silence. Al experiences a stab of
frustration that he cannot see what is happening, but
then again, maybe it is for the best, he still seems to
be plagued with jealous.

Finally, they advance towards the chairs and
window seat.

And so, here they are, finally alone, cloistered in her
luxurious bedroom, of rose marble and golden,
lemon trim.

"You really must go?"

"There is no reason for me to remain here,"

Both men register the reaction on the young woman's countenance.

"No, I didn't mean that. You know what I mean," Erik is drowning, trying to recuperate his blunder.

Angelique laughs.

"Silly, I know what you mean. Your place is with your father."

"But you do believe me when I promise that there is no plot against your father, no secret army or anything?"

"I believe you."

"But why would Arthur be so sure of such a thing?"

"You know that he still hasn't forgiven him for welcoming Lancelot and Guinevere. He still judges your father partly responsible for what happened."

"But that was so long ago, I was only a baby then. And why now? There is something more to it. There has to be someone else that wishes to attack Galahaut.

Could Arthur be plotting with Mordred to take over our lands?"

"No, Arthur would never do such a thing, he trusts not cousin Mordred, nor his evil sister Morgan le Fey, they have betrayed him more than once."

"So, who else might benefit from weakening my father? For without the Sceptre, he would be defenceless against any attack using magic."

"Other than Morgan, the only other magician that would be strong enough to do any real harm, would be Merlin, and why would he think to do such a thing?"

Erik shakes his head, hunches his shoulders, and sighs a heavy sigh.

"Who-ever. It changes not the facts, without its protection, anyone with enough knowledge of magic, would be a dangerous threat."

"Then you shall have it back." She gets up, maybe to emphasis her affirmation, maybe mark the end of this interview.

Al's whole attention is fixed on every sign, every muscle twitch, on that exquisite face.

"I know what has to be done, I shall charge myself with this heavy mission."

The jaw is firm and decided, but the deep, deep
emerald eyes, could no more mask her sorrow, than
a chimp might mask an elephant.

The sorrow of the knowledge, that theirs was an
impossible love, that even their being here now,
together has put them both in unspeakable danger.

"Hurry, you must leave, I will send word when it is
done,"

And so, the silent shadow, once again, melts from
her sight, leaving an immense empty space in her
room, and in her heart.

Al then makes himself a comfortable space amongst
the spare bedding on the floor of the wardrobe, to
patiently wait for her to leave for supper, so that he
too, can melt into the dark shadows…

Ch. 31 Clarity and Secrecy

Al is troubled, he knows that he was kidnapped, that there was a ransom letter and the contents thereof. He also trusts both Erik and Angelique, and Galahaut has always proven himself to be man of honour.

And now this.

A letter that was sent to him.

It was delivered by one of the castle servants.

He didn't know the lady that gave it to him, just that she said that it was most important he would get it, and no one else must know.

She had given him a groat, and then hurried away.

The letter simply said:
'You know that the sceptre does not belong here. You must do everything that you can to return it to where it should be.' Signed; 'a friend'.

It was troubling, things just didn't add up.

He is also aware that his lady, is likely to try and steal the sceptre, and, not being a trained thief, is also likely to get herself caught and into trouble.

Now, that adds up, it adds up to something awful.

Finally, he cannot tell anyone any of this, as, if the king were to hear of his talking about being a spy, and what he knew, there would be a real risk of having his tongue cut out.

If only there was someone that he could trust, one hundred percent to keep his secret.

Someone who's very life depended on keeping secrets.

Someone of the church.

He has waited until after lunch, when he knows that Friar Brendan takes his afternoon stroll, or more correctly afternoon nap, in the gardens.

"Father, could I talk with you for a moment?"

"Eh? What?" The plump priest blinks his eyes open.

He was enjoying the soft, warm scented air. The sun on his face, and the fullness of his belly.

"Oh, hello Alain, what can I do for you?"

"I have something important to talk about, but it must be in the strictest of secrecy."

The older man slowly gets up and starts peering into the bushes.

"I don't think that anyone is small enough to hide in there."

"I'm not looking for people, I'm looking for birds."

"Birds?"

"Yes, yellow eyed birds."

"And why are you looking for yellow eyed birds?"

"Because, young man, witches and wizards have an irritating habit of using birds to spy on people. And the only sign that they have bewitched the poor thing, is that their eyes turn yellow."

"Well there's no birds here, none at all."

"Then we're good then, Come sit with me, and lighten your soul."

And so, to the very best of his abilities, Al recounts all that has happened since he left the tavern of his adoptive parents, so many moons ago.

"… and so I don't know what to think, I trust both Lord Erik and the Lady Angelique, but I cannot imagine why or how King Arthur could get us to steal the magical sceptre."

"Revenge, as you have suggested might be a motivation, but why to have waited so long to act, and how to have orchestrated all this is quite beyond me.

Power is another great motivator, but would he have any interest in attacking and subjugating Galahaut, again, I have only questions but no answers."

"Power, the sceptre doesn't give power, but stops the power of others."

"Only against magical attacks."

"So having it neutralises someone else's power."

"Only if they were a powerful witch or wizard."

"And there is only one powerful wizard, here in Camelot." Al seems to be having an epiphany.

"Are you suggesting that Merlin is behind or this?" The friar becomes much more tonic.

"No, I'm not suggesting, now, I know." There is an assurance in his tone.

"How do you know?"

"The Copper Knight, he could only have been created by use of some very powerful magic, the same as the mirror of the past."

"But to what aim?"

"So as to weaken Lancelot's spirit. By revisiting his past and having a very critical conscience underlining every error that he had made, he would feel uncertain of himself. Then, in a moment of questioning, where would he go, who would he seek out, only his best friend, Galahaut?"

"Go on." The priest is intrigued.

"There was a seagull on the boat with yellow eyes."

"Seagulls have very small eyes, and yellow beaks, you could have been mistaken."

"The kidnappers knew where we were, but there was a bird that was singing, flying towards us."

"Not all birds are controlled by wizards."

"They threatened to throw me off the cliff, but there were two beds ready for us."

"They must of just been trying to frighten you, you said that they wanted you to deliver the scroll."

"Then there were bats in the tower. They also had yellow eyes."

"Maybe they were just light brown, there was not much light to see"

"And the whole thing about giving me the letter and leaving me alone with time to read it, and then to escape."

"They couldn't know that you could read."

"Do you think that Merlin doesn't?"

"Well maybe." He admits, thoughtfully.

"And the noises that Dena was making in the back of the cart, I couldn't believe that Michael didn't hear them."

"When you are listening for something, it always seems louder."

"And the two messengers, both people that we would have confidence in. …"

"Only logical."

"That stopped us confronting Galahaut about the letter."

"So not to alert him that you were aware of his plans."

"But how would Arthur have found out about it all?"

"Because Arthur has spies." The good friar is showing signs of exhaustion and, if anything, boredom.

"And, and, and the owl."

"What owl?"

"Oh, I forgot, the ambush, where Lancelot got hit on the head."

"What about it?"

"An owl warned us. I clearly remember that it had yellow eyes."

"Seriously? And why after all that he has done to thwart you, would he suddenly decide to help?"

"Because, because he needed us to keep the sceptre, he couldn't risk that someone else would steal it from us. Also, maybe it wasn't just by chance that Faron and company would arrive to save us, in the last minute."

"How so?"

"They could have been told to follow us back to Camelot, to make sure that we didn't change our minds and think to return it to Galahaut. If we did, then they would have been the ones to ambush us, and steal back the sceptre."

"All this seems pretty far-fetched."

"And, only Merlin or Morgan are likely to have interest in acquiring the sceptre, no one else could have an interest in Galahaut or in the protection against magic."

"You cannot be sure of that."

"No, but it makes sense. And if Merlin wanted to manipulate King Arthur into getting it back, with his smouldering hatred against Galahaut, it wouldn't be difficult to convince him that he was amassing a secret army."

"Listen, I understand your wish to believe that the father of Dena is innocent of any plot.

And that you are afraid that the Lady Angelique could, through her love of the Duke, find herself doing something that she will regret.

But that is not enough to convince me of your version of this story."

"Thank you. father, but I don't need to convince you of this. I only need to convince one person of the truth."

"And who might that be?"

"The person that you are talking to." Al smiles, bows, and takes his leave.

Ch. 32 The Band of Thieves

It is taken a certain amount of time to convince Marion and Jay to agree to help.

Marion was easier to convince, but Jay, always protective of his safety and wellbeing, was a harder nut to crack.

Finally, Al had to threaten him, that if he didn't help, then there would be no reason for either of them to keep the secret of his 'new' name and origins.

From his two new conspirators he learned that only Merlin or a person, highly trusted by the king, could get into the tower room and take the sceptre.

Angelique was planning to steal it the very next night as there was to be a meeting of the round table and both the king and the magician would be present.

Marion was to distract the guard, while she would go and get the staff.

However, the problem was getting it out of the castle.

All the doors and windows of the lower floors had been blocked by a powerful spell.

A spell cast by Merlin, to stop anyone other than himself from taking it out of the building.

Hoping that she would somehow find a solution to this, she had already planned to meet Erik at the abandoned village, some miles out from Camelot.

That was all the he needed.

He warned Marion to not let Angelique leave her room after she had taken the sceptre. He himself would find the means to get it out of the castle.

He then hurried off to his father's tavern, expecting to find some old friends drinking there.

Faron is sitting in a corner taking a quiet drink.

He shows some surprise to see the young squire approach him.

"Faron, I need your help."

"I's tired, no work f' now. Y' can find som'un else. An' thanks for askin'."

"Faron, I need you and your team for a few hours tomorrow night, it's important."

"Wha's so important?"

"The sceptre, it was stolen by mistake."

"Mistake?"

"Yes, and it needs to be returned where it belongs."

"And 'ow is we t' do that?"

"You will need to get into the castle and come to a place on the third level. From there, you will need to take it out from a window and bring it down to the ground.

Then, I will come back and get it from you."

"You'll give us the thing on the third floor, we takes it out o' the eyethurl, climb down the wall, an' you meets us at the bottom?

I though it wus the knight that got 'is skull caved in, not you. Why not jus' walks out wi' it under your tunic?"

There is a magic spell that stops anyone taking it out from the first two floors. No one has thought that someone would take it out from higher up."

"Okay, sounds like a job, but who'll be payin' us?"

"I will see that you get well paid. You can trust me."

Faron stops for a short moment to consider.

"Handband." He stands up.

Al solemnly takes the hand of the crook. They are now honour-bound to keep their word and their bargain.

Ch. 33 The Second Theft

The lady Angelique is a little surprised to see the squire entering her chambers.

"Prey, to what purpose might you be here?" She inquires, surely, a little put-out to have this young man entering into her private quarters.

Al looks towards Marion, she half shrugs and then looks away. She has not wanted to say anything more before being sure that he would appear.

"Madame, I have come to take the sceptre to Duke Erik."

"And just what sceptre might you be referring to?" She responds in a cold, icy tone.

"The one that you have stolen tonight. We do not have much time for this. Marion," he turns to his unwilling accomplice, "please convince your mistress that I am here in good faith."

"Well, Marion, is he to be trusted?"

"Yes ma'am, Al is to be trusted. I've known him all our lives, and he has never lied or stolen anything." She then stops for a moment, only to correct herself.

"Well, other than having help to steal the sceptre, in the first place."

"Yes, we must not forget that, should we?" But she is smiling.

"I could never rest if the king were to find out that you had stolen it. I have a plan to get it out of the castle."

"But all the doors and windows have been sealed."

"Yes, I am aware of that, but only the first two floors. We can take it out of one of the higher levels."

"And who can we trust to do such a thing?"

A valid question. He takes a long moment before deciding to answer.

"The same thieves that stole it from Galahaut."

"And you trust them?"

"They gave their hand."

"And you think that makes them trustworthy?"

"They are doing this for money. If they don't do as I ask, then they won't get paid."

"They could think to tell the king, he might reward them, and there would be no risk."

"I'm sure that Galahaut will pay well to get his sceptre back, and they must know that."

"So, I am to entrust the sceptre to you?"

"I will see that it arrives in the hands of the Duke."

Now it is her turn to hesitate. She turns again to Marion for support, she nods to her mistress, and Angelique nods in turn.

"Give it to him. And may the Virgin protect your steps." And with that, she turns and goes to sit, facing the window. She no longer has any part in this story.

Marion goes to the cupboard and extracts an object, the sceptre is swathed in a silken scarf.

Al carefully takes the bundle, the scarf smells of his Lady. Somehow, he will find a way to steal that scarf for himself.

After all, he deserves something for his troubles.

He slips out of her chambers, across the small hall and down a series of steps,

Arriving on the third-floor corridor, he finds to his great relief, that Faron is already there. He is escorted by Jay, who has walked him in through the servant's entry, and directed him to here.

Faron is alone, which surprises Al somewhat, as he presumed that he would bring Michael to scale down the wall.

"You're alone?"

" 'S right. Got the stick?"

"Here." He passes over the sceptre.

Faron digs out a large sack and pulls out a pile of rags, a quantity of straw escapes with them. As the sack still shows signs of being half full, Al assumes that there is a bed of straw covering the bottom of the container.

The crook wraps the sceptre in layers of cloth before placing it into the rough, woven receptacle.

He then heaves the sack out of the window and slowly lowers it down, using a long rope which is attached. After a while, he changes his technique and counts three hand changes, and waits a moment, then another three, and then wait.

After a number of these manoeuvres they hear a low whistle from outside.

"Done. D'know why's you needed us to do that. Easy money f' droppin' a sack out o' an eyethurl."

Jay looks across to Al.

"And you're supposed to be so clever," and slowly shakes his head.

Ch. 34. The Bold Squire.

Al leads his horse, already saddled and ready, out of the stables and leads him round to the side of the castle.

Duncan is there, waiting for him, bundle in hand. It is still swathed in the rags brought by Faron.

The young man smiles and nods to the lanky, red-headed acrobat, and takes the valuable merchandise.

Once safely some distance from the castle, he mounts his steed and trots off.

Once undercover of the first clump of trees, he takes the time to unwrap the sceptre, take her scarf and secrete it in his tunic, before re- binding it in the sackcloth.

Then continues towards the abandoned village.

The wind was a torrent of darkness among the gusty
trees.
The moon was a ghostly galleon tossed upon cloudy seas.
The road was a ribbon of moonlight over the purple
moor,
And the bold squire came riding—
        Riding—riding— riding
The bold squire came riding, up to the old inn-door.

He slid from his trusty stallion, and dropped onto the ground.
The ghosts of lonesome trav'lers, they whispered all around
His hand was on his dagger, as he heard the boots behind
He'd looked for him by moonlight,
        And come for him by moonlight,
He came for him by moonlight, now knowing what he'd find.

Not a word by them was spoken, there were no words to say
The spectres watched in silence, this game of end of day
He turned 'round to the saddle, to draw the sceptre out
His back was clear in the moonlight
….. Defenceless, in the moonlight,
He could die here in the moonlight, of that there is no doubt.

He turns with the prize to the other, his anger would force to kill,
He hands him over the sceptre, the enemy, just stands still
He hesitates to take it, he knows the cost to bear,
They stand there in moonlight,
……. Together in the moonlight,
To share the taste of triumph, and smell the scent of fear.

He takes the packaged object, ne'er a word is spoke
The spirits fly around them, but silence never broke.
He climbs back on the saddle, he knows what is in store,
And the bold squire left riding—
        Riding—riding— riding
And the bold squire left riding, back over the purple moor.

Ch. .35 Morning is Broken

Al passes a troubled night, full of nightmares, huge flying, yellow eyed creatures, swooping towards him.

Penning him against a wall.

Then the wall is in the chamber of the round table, and all the knights are there, Arthur and Merlin.

Merlin has the Copper Knight's magic mirror, and all can see him passing over the sceptre to Duke Erik.

The nobles are all banging on the table, 'Guilty, guilty, guilty'. Sir Lancelot, sitting next the king, is shouting the loudest.

Al drags himself, miserably out from his sleeping corner.

Quietly passing the peaceful, sleeping form of his master, he makes his way down to the kitchen.

Not being able to sleep, at least he can benefit to purloin himself some hot, freshly baked bread and a slab of cheese, to cheer himself up.

As they say, 'the best laid schemes o' mice an' men, ang aft a-gley', yes, they certainly, often go awry.

He is just about to savour his first mouthful, when his well-planned breakfast is rudely interrupted by the arrival of the palace guards.

"Everyone, you are to immediately stop anything that you are doing and come with us."

Al does not protest, not like the cook who screams at the guards that there is food cooking and she cannot leave the kitchen.

The guards seem a little confused and someone leaves to confer with the captain of the guards.

The squire profits from this moment of confusion to take several bites of bread and cheese, and then to wrap them in a cloth and stuff them down his tunic.

He is a little confused to realise that there is already something hiding in there.

Until he remembers Angelique's scarf, and smiles to himself, just knowing that it is there.

The solution is to give the cook several minutes to take the food off of the fire and to order that the food that needs to be kept cool, to be restocked in the pantry.

They then allow themselves to be herded out into the courtyard.

All of the castle servants are penned together, surrounded by the palace guards.

After some moments of waiting and confusion, the royal party arrives.

"Look, look, it's Merlin," someone remarks, "Merlin has come too, it must be really important."

From out of the crowd, Lancelot appears, and approaches the rostrum.

No one thinks to stop him climbing onto the stage.

His attention is initially focused on Arthur, but he looks 'round in the direction of Merlin.

It is difficult to read his reaction when his eyes fall on the person of the royal magician.

Any reflection would be interrupted by the King who begins to speak.

"Most of you will not be aware of why you are here. Some of you might suspect. And one or some of you will know well. I will make this short and as painless as possible.

If the person or persons that stole the Uffington Sceptre, do not reveal themselves immediately, I will treat each and every one of you as thieves, with the usual consequences."

 "They will brand us on the shoulder and chop off our right hands." Someone explains to one of the youngest stable boys, freshly arrived from another part of the country.

"You cannot be serious?" He responds, terror flashing in his wide, brown eyes.

"That is the law here."

"But all of us? Maybe none of us did it."

"It looks like someone did." He points his flabby arm towards someone else in the crowd.

Someone is pushing his way forward.

Someone who pushes his way through the guards, who think not to impede him.

Pushing his way directly towards the royal podium.

"I did it your majesty. I will take all punishment. I acted totally alone and without any help or support from anyone in the palace."

Lancelot looks totally shocked, he cannot believe what he is seeing or hearing.

"Squire, do you realise what you are saying?" The King was also, clearly, a little taken aback.

"Yes your Majesty, I stole the sceptre and I personally returned it to the Duke Erik of Sorelais.

I firmly believe that there is no secret army, and therefore no surprise attack against Camelot planned.

I believe that without the sceptre, King Galahaut will be invaded by the Picts, under the command of Mordred.

These are my motives, for which I have done this deed. And I repeat that I acted on my own initiative, by myself and alone."

"But of course that is not possible," Merlin speaks to the King, and all listen.

"The sceptre was in your own chambers, protected by certain spells, only a person that you have confidence in would have access to it."

"Sire, you expressed confidence in me, it must have been enough to allow me access to your chambers and take the sceptre." Al lies without either hesitation or the least signs of stutter.

"Who else, apart from members of the royal household would your incantations have allowed to gain my private apartments?"

"That would be a question I would need to reflect on."

"But it was I, m'lord. You need not seek further."

"And, even if you did, how would you have gotten it out of the castle?"

"Sire, you have given me free access and egress to and from the castle. I simply lowered it down with a rope from an upper floor, before slipping out to find it, t'was an easy enough task."

"Well, Merlin, what think you?"

"I doubt that he would do such a thing without the knowledge and support of his master."

"Sire, if I might speak."

Please, please Lady Angelique, please do not say anything to implicate yourself.

"Speak daughter."

"Lancelot was the brave knight that stole the sceptre for you in the first place. His loyalty to you as King has never been in question.

If he had had a change of heart, we would have heard him speak of it. He is not capable to let his squire, a mere boy, take the punishment for an act, direct or indirect of his."

"I have spoken often with the good knight, and never has he ever suggested the possibility of returning the sceptre," He had not noticed the good friar joining the royal party.

"Thank you, father, thank you daughter. Sir Lancelot, what do you have to say on this matter?"

"Sire, I am as shocked and surprised as you are. I would never have thought that he could do such a thing. And I swear an oath on God and my honour as a knight, that I had no idea **what-so-ever** that this was planned or carried out."

Arthur stops for a single moment. Merlin slowly shakes his head.

"Sir Lancelot, you have never lied, for all that you might have done, you are a man of honour, I will take your word that you have had no part in this."

217

To turns back to Al. "And you, villain, you know what fate awaits you?"

"My fate is in your hands, sire." There is nothing else to do but wait and hope that the king will be merciful. His right hand will surely be forfeit.

"And the blood of all Camelot will be on yours, boy. You will be hanged tomorrow, hanged until you are died, and then left until the crows have totally devoured your putrid flesh. Let that be a warning to all, no one steals from the royal household!"

And there it was.

Ch. 36. Final Words

"But why?"

They are in the cold, damp cell at the bottom of the donjon tower. Lancelot has come to visit his erstwhile squire.

He is having a difficult time understanding the motives of the young man.

"I've already told you, just as I told the King, I believed Duke Erik, and I believe that Mordred without the protection of the sceptre, would have mounted an attack against Galahaut, and would have destroyed him."

"But why would Arthur want to see Galahaut destroyed?" The obvious question.

"Remember, politics?" Al reminds him.

"So you also believe in the evil intent of King Arthur?" He is trying not to accept the possibility of evil intentions of his sovereign.

"Sire, you are a knight of the round table, of the court of King Arthur. It is your sacred duty to follow him as your King. I will not go to my grave thinking that I have put doubt into your mind about your liege."

"You are willing to die for this?" Relieved to be able to let the matter drop, he is still feeling troubled.

"I have no choice."

'Either I accept this alone, or all the others will share in my fate. And it would not be clear if I would have any better outcome,' he reflects.

"You are a most honourable young man." A warm glow awakens in the very depths of the innocent robber.

"Remember me with fondness, for I have been privileged to serve you." He smiles bravely to the knight and salutes him.

"Goodbye, Al," returning the salute, he goes to excuse himself from the heavy moment.

"Goodbye, Sir Lancelot, please do not come tomorrow." It would be too difficult to look into his eyes in those last instants.

"As you wish." Could that be relief that he reads in his face?

"It is as I wish." Either way, it will be easier for both of them if he would not be there.

"Goodbye."

"Goodbye."

He turns abruptly and leaves the cell, leaving Al alone to face his final hours.

However, he is not alone for all that long.

"Would you wish to make your final confession, Alain?"

The holy father is sad and troubled, it is his duty to facilitate the boy to reach his Father in heaven. Such, Al easily imagines, are the thoughts of he that has brought him to Camelot, so many moons ago.

"Father, I have nothing to confess. I believe that I have done that which is right."

"You must confess your sins, any sin left un-repented could bar your access to heaven."

"There, there is one thing."

"Something that I stole."

"The sceptre." He offers, helpfully.

"No, no, I already said, that is not something that I'm ashamed of, that was something that I had to do. Something that, something that I'm, I'm proud to have done."

"Then, then what have you stolen, that you are repenting for?"

"This," and he pulls out the perfumed scarf.

"That is a lady's scarf," Al passes it over to him. "A lady of the house?"

"The scarf belongs to the Lady Angelique. Please do not tell anyone of this, please just return it to her."

"Where did you get this scarf?"

"I stole it."

"Why would you steal her scarf?" He is having difficulty understanding the act.

"I would rather not tell you."

"Alain, this is your final confession. If you do not confess all, you will go to hell."

"This is not something for me to confess. I have confessed that I have stolen the scarf. For that I will accept my penance. Anything more than that is not my story, my sin ends there, I can say no more."

"Ten 'Hail Mary's', and your theft of the scarf will be absolved."

"Thank you, father. Father?"

"Yes, my son. Please ask for my family to not come, I cannot deal with seeing them suffer."

"I will pass on your message. Anything else?"

"Yes."

He waits patiently to hear this last request.

"Could you please be there with me, I'm so, so scared." And the innocent young man dissolves into tears.

His spiritual father, holds his ward, and gently rocks him to sleep.

And so, the long night begins, …

… but tomorrow will be another day.

Ch. 37 Another Day.

He didn't remember the prison cot being so soft, but then again, he had never slept in this room before, maybe it is just a final dream.

It is the cock crowing that has woken him up, and so it is.

He drags himself out of bed, throws on his clothes, and walks over to washing bowl.

He could just splash some fresh water onto his face, but can't really be bothered, so he just dunks his head in it.

Faron looks up and catches his reflection in the mirror.

It is the face of Lancelot that is staring back at him.

"Fucking weird dream,"

He turns to the hidden alcove and calls out.

"Come on Al, wake up you lazy bastard, don't think
that I'm going to let you sleep all day."

Since there is no answer, he walks over to
investigate, but finds the sleeping corner
uninhabited.

Shrugging his shoulders, he makes for the door,
ready for a good breakfast.

Opening the door, he is surprised to find Jay,
propped up against the facing wall.

He must having been sleeping there all night, and
the opening of the door would have woken him up.

"Sire?"

"Yes?"

"Sire, we must do something, we cannot let him
die."

"Who, let who die?"

"Al, Al will be hanged today. Hanged at noon, in
front of the whole village. We have to do
something."

'Fuck, it wasn't just a dream. Yes, yes of course I
remember, But how could I know all of …?'

Faron realises that he has experienced that which he had asked the guide to let him live through.

In one long night, he has shared months and months of Al's reality.

"Find me Father Brendan, and be quick about it," but needn't have bothered to direct him to hasten.

In an instant, he is gone, as fast as any magical being.

Puck's response to Oberon's order, resonates in his head; "I'll put a girdle round about the earth, in forty minutes."

'I doubt that I could be patient for forty minutes,' he reflects on returning to his chambers.

The fat friar arrives several minutes later, carrying a number of sweet rolls in his pudgy hand. He must have been interrupted during an important meeting with his breakfast.

"What has happened?"

"Have *you*, now lost *your* memory?"

"What are you speaking of?"

"Everything."

"Yes, yes, of course, now you must know."

"Yes, I know everything. I know who I am, I know who Lancelot is, and I know why Al stole the sceptre."

"And that he is to be hanged at noon."

"So, what are we going to do about it?"

"What-ever you wish to, or not, as the case may be.

You shouldn't forget that this is only your creation, a projection, nothing here is real, Al does not really exit."

Faron stops for a moment to consider this.

"As long as this reality, created by me exists, everyone in it, experiences life as real."

"And?"

"And they are capable to feel, to know pain, to suffer."

"Is that a statement or a question?"

"It is my experience of these worlds."

"Then, I suppose that you are right."

"If I do nothing, them Al will hang. And he will go through the real agony of having his life chocked out of his young body."

"But if you do anything to save the boy, you will put into peril your relationship with Arthur, and most likely, dash any chance of fulfilling your relationship with the Lady Angelique."

"So, you would suggest that I just let him die, and carry on with this modern-day version of 'A Connecticut Yankee in King Arthur's Court'?"

"I don't suggest anything, I am just hoping to help to guide you in your decision-making process."

Faron puts his head in his hands and roughly rubs his face.

"Fuck! And I'd chosen to stop worrying about 'doing-the-right-thing' years ago. And, the fucking cherry on the cake, for someone that only exists as a figment of my own imagination."

He sighs heavily and goes to the door. Jay is hanging around waiting to see what will happen.

"Please find Marion and ask the Lady Angelique to meet us in her chambers as soon as possible. … Wait! And when you've delivered my message, go to the kitchens and get us both some bread and cheese, I'm famished."

Jay stops for the merest of moments, integrating the two commands and then turns to hurry off and fulfil the master's wishes.

"So, you have chosen to intervene?"

"No." The priest looks confused.

"No, I have decided that *we* shall intervene. This time, you are going to take an active role in the proceedings."

"But, I cannot do that."

"Oh yes you can, and you will."

At that moment the discussion is interrupted by the return of the page. He is ladened down with a heavy tray loaded with bread, meat, cheese and two mugs of some type of liquid.

"What's all this?"

"I might have mentioned that you would be trying to do something for Al, and that you wished for something to eat and drink…" He smiles, sheepishly.

He sets the tray down on the low table in the centre of the chamber.

"You did say that I might also eat some of the food?" He is standing quite some distance away from the enticing fare.

Lancelot laughs at the young man.

"Come, we will likely need all the sustenance that we can get, this might prove to be a rather trying day.

Ch. 38 A Council of War

Faron has not, up until now, felt the full assurance of Sir Lancelot, Knight of the Round Table.

He knows that he is going to end his relationship with Arthur, with this incarnation of his dead father, for ever. Again, rejected and despised, again, any hope of respect and appreciation, totally ruined.

And, to add insult to injury, his chance of building a healthy, loving union with Angelique, is about to be kicked, a long, long way into touch.

But he is Lancelot, and there is no choice, Al must be saved. He has lived that innocent yet noble life. He cannot be allowed to suffer the pain of being hanged.

No matter the personal sacrifice, they will try, whatever they might, to save the youth's life.

So, here he is, with Friar Brendan and Jay, on tow, marching, purposefully towards Lady Angelique's chambers.

Discretely, but firmly, he taps on her door.

Faron is slightly surprised to find that it his daughter Aideen that answers.

"Maid Marian, please may we entre?" He has certainly not forgotten his manners.

It suddenly occurs to our modern hero, that the knight must somehow have access to some of his memories, at least those that he has, that include Al's vision of the last months.

The princess is standing, next to an ornately wrought wood and metal table.

"Sire, by what right doth thou think to order me to my chambers, and invade them without so much as a 'by-your-leave'?"

"By the right of good and God. My squire is to be hanged. He is the most loyal and noble person that I have ever had the good fortune to encounter."

He is in this situation because he wished to right the wrong that I had committed, and to protect you from your implication is this risky affair."

"How do you …?" But she never thought to finish her question. It is obvious that, somehow, the knight is aware of all that has passed, or at least, enough of it to incriminate her in this.

And so, high breeding coming to the rescue, she stops
and turns towards her maid.

"Please see that everyone is seated, and we shall discuss
the problem."

Everyone, clearly did not include Jay or herself.

Then.
"Does anyone have any idea as to how we might set
about this?"

Faron stops, he is not good at finding answers when put
on the spot. Fortunately, as always, there is someone to
step in, and save him.

Jay coughs delicately.

They all turn to the young page.

And he explains exactly how, Al is to be rescued.

Ch. 39 The Magic Trick

The holy friar and his five hooded postulants are sitting in a secluded corner of the tavern.

There is only one thing that spreads quicker than the plague, gossip.

They were not the only one's to have travelled from Camelot that day.

He was holding court by the roaring fire.

"Again," someone insisted, "I's didn't catch it all."

"Me flagon's empty, can't talk wiv' a dry throat."

"Here, this one's on the house," the innkeeper was also enjoying the entertainment.

"Well, this is exactly what the guard 'e said, word f' word.

So, first, the friar 'e comes down to hear the last words of the thief. He spends some time for the last confession, and then he goes.

So, says the guard, 'e looks troubled, that's 'is own words, troubled, the holy father is troubled.

Then 'e 'ears someone coming down the stairs, 'e is waiting for the others t' come and take the lad out, but it's not them, it's a woman. She's dressed in a riding cloak, with a hood coverin' 'er 'ead.

'You can't be here,' says the guard, pullin' 'is sword.

'I need to see him,' she says, and pulls down the hood.

By our Lady, if it's not the princess Angelique?

Now what business is it of hers to be visitin' condemned prisoners?

I'll tell you why she'd be there.

'E's done an' given that magic stick to the Duke Erik, and she's a bloody good friend of 'is.

So there she is, just gone into his cell, when another runs down after her. She's also wearin' a long ridin' cape, and 'er 'ead 'idden under 'er 'ood.

She takes the 'ood down for a second, and 'e recognises 'er, it's 'er lady-in-waitin'

So, she follows 'er into the prison, and almost straight way, 'er ladyship comes out.

'I just wanted to say goodbye. He did what he thought was right. Come Marion, let's leave this sad place. If the horses are ready, we will leave immediately.'

'Coming ma'am,' she shouts from inside and then runs out of the cell, with 'er hood back up, and rushes up the stairs after 'er mistress.

At last, the guards come to take 'im out to the gallows, but no, it's not.

It's the Knight Lancelot, come to say a final farewell to his untrustworthy squire.

'But what's this?'

The guard rushes to cell, only to find …" He stops, dramatically, to take a long drink of mead.

"The boy is no longer there. It's the lady-in-waiting, dressed in the boy's clothes, crying, 'let me go, let me go.'

So, 'e calls f' the captain o' the guards, and 'e says to let 'er out.

An' she says that she was ridin' with the Lady Angelique, an' then, all goes black, and then she opens 'er eyes, and 'ere she is, locked up in me cell.

'This must be the work o' Morgan Le Fay', swears the knight, 'she's the only magician powerful enough to switch people.

And now the sceptre is away from Camelot, she's rescued 'er thief. Now we knows that it wus 'er that wus behind the theft.'

So now's everyone lookin' for the boy, but no-one's seen sight nor sound of 'im, 'es jus' vanished.

'Ow can a boy, all alone jus' vanish? 'S'truth, 'tis magic."

Faron is enjoying hearing the traveller's version of events.

Of course, it was nothing more than a simple conjurer's trick of sleight of hand.

One that they had Jay to thank for.

The friar brings down a dress of Marion's, they are of about the same size.

Angelique then comes down coving her face, supposedly, so no-one would see that she was coming to visit.

So, when Marian follows down, wearing a cloak and hiding her face, the guard takes that as normal.

She follows Angelique into the cell and passes her cloak to Al, he puts it on, while the princess is talking to the guard, informing him that she is going to leave the palace and go riding.

Al has already removed his own clothes and put on the dress similar to that of Marion.

Now hidden in the cloak and hood, he rushes out of the cell and up the stairs. The guard notices nothing unusual, the switch is made.

Jay is waiting just outside the donjon with two horses, and off they go. No one thinks to look too closely at the hooded rider accompanying the Lady Angelique, out for a ride.

While waiting for Lancelot to arrive, Marion has ample time to remove her dress and to put on Al's clothes.

The knight arrives, grabs her dress and conceals it under his jerkin.

The guard does not notice the few seconds between his arriving and his calling for aid.

To oversee the release of Marion and confirm that this is an act of the worst witchcraft, takes little time.

After Lancelot had discovered the magical switching of Al and Marion, he had planned to leave alone and meet Al at the crossroads leading to the South.

What he hadn't anticipated was Jay and Marian insisting on joining him, as he parted from the castle.

And if that wasn't unexpected enough, to then find Friar Brendan and Angelique flanking Al, that was just more than he could ever have fantasised.

So here they all are, hooded and cloaked disciples, on their way to join some vague sounding religious order. Under the ever-watchful eyes of the good father Brendan.

This adventure is finally threatening to be … fun!

Ch. 40 Heading North

To avoid the obvious and shortest route to the North, which Arthur would surely have had blocked, they skirted the South coast for a while, before finally turning their horses away from the channel.

Faron, was surprised to pass through towns that knew the names of; Winchester, Abington, Oxford, (of course), Northampton, Coventry, Lichfield, Manchester and over to Pul.

It was only when they were riding along the coast road, the same as Lancelot rode, when tracking and rescuing Guinevere, that it strikes Faron where he is.

The ancient town of Pul, is nothing other than the famous Lancashire holiday resort, now known as Blackpool.

Blackpool, Blackpool, Blackpool.

A flood of forgotten memories wash over his consciousness.

For, you see, he has been here before, yes, as Al, following Lancelot's memories, but also as himself, as Faron.

Somewhere between being seven and ten years old.

J.J. had wanted to come to this sea-side resort to see, first hand, how some party, political conference was happening.

As, it was the summer holidays and Marie Madeleine was wanting to take some time off, Maman had suggested that *les garçons* might enjoy the experience.

Of course. that meant that she would have the house to herself for a whole week, to do Lord knows what.

His father, didn't see any problem there, and so they were packed up and sent off with him to the diamond of the North-West coast.

Not having any idea where to stay, and not wanting to waste good money on an expensive hotel, he had asked if any of the workers in his factory had any suggestions. One of his technicians, named Harry Burke, had a relative that went annually to very nice, little, inexpensive boarding house.

It was, 'North Shore', not very far on one side from the train station, and on the other side from the sea. There was also a crazy golf course, not far.

Faron smiles to himself, as he remembers asking the woman that ran the little hotel if they would be having bacon and eggs for breakfast.

How she smiled and promised that he would be having
something much, much better, worsht and eggs.

J.J. had taken them to the pleasure-beach, one of the
biggest amusement parks in Europe. He had found an
open bar, piled them with money and allowed them to run
riot.

Of course, they stuffed themselves like crazy, Faron
throw up after one of the rides. Jay, who might have been
a little more reasonable, succeeded not to.

There was a lounge built in the cellar of the boarding
house, where there was music and games every evening.

The owners had three sons, but two had already left
home. The third, he remembered, was very kind and
patient and was happy to entertain the two brothers.

However, what touched Faron the most, was the
grandfather.

The grandfather was a tailor, who lived and worked in a
little house and shop on the next road.

During the day that J.J. went to the conference, they were
offered the possibility to go and see this venerable person
at work.

Jay didn't really fancy, he had bought a pile of comic
books and was eager to start to devoir them.

So, Faron was escorted to the old man's tailor-shop. They passed through the shop part and then back into the cosy workroom.

The first surprise was that about a third of the room was taken by an enormous table. And sitting, cross-legged was this old, old man, sewing.

He smiled at the young boy and gestured for him to climb up and sit beside him.

Faron, fell into some sort of a trance.

There was a radio playing, the tailor smoked cigarette sized cigars, and Faron just sat and watched.

At some point of the morning he was shown where the toilet was, and around lunchtime, a small, quite fat woman brought them down bowls of chicken soup, bread, and Coca-Cola.

Faron has tried various techniques of meditation, at different moments of his life, but nothing could come close to the energy of this master.

"Come!"

Faron is shocked out of reverie by the call of a boats-man.

He leads them to the jetty where they have to manoeuvre their horses over a narrow ramp to get them onto the boat.

To finally arrive on the ferry, without having encountered any of Arthur's men, feels like some sort of a miracle.

In a few hours they will be back under Galahaut's protection, and then they will finally be safe.

The crossing was easy and uneventful, and one could almost feel the mounting excitement as they started the approach towards the island's port.

"Look, look, Galahaut, he's here, he's come to greet us." Faron smiles, even Jay can show some enthusiasm, when he felt like it.

Not only was the king present, but it seemed that most of the royal guard had also come to welcome the weary travellers.

Impatiently, they wait for the boat to dock and the landing planks to be put into place.

One by one, carefully leading their horses they disembark the vessel.

Something starts to worry Lancelot, Faron can feel his body start to tense up.

What has he noticed?

Not one of the welcoming party has moved, and Galahaut is not smiling.

But, before he has a chance to act, the king advances.

"Arrest them! I don't know how you can think to dare to come here, but don't expect to leave while you still have breath in your lungs."

Ch. 41 Changing Alliances

"Wait, they's not t' blame." A raggedy man runs out of the crowd.

Faron has no trouble identifying him, after all, he has spent forty years looking at his face in the mirror.

"And just who might this be?" Galahaut is not amused.

"Me name is Faron, your majesty." One of the knights goes and whispers in his ear.

"What? What kind of insanity is this? You are the rogue that stole the sceptre from me?"

"Ay," he sighs slightly, "that would be me." The knight jumps down off his horse, runs towards the thief, drawing his sword, as he does so.

"Wait!" Now it is the turn of the young squire to run forward. He stops in front of the acrobat, blocking the sword with his own body.

"Wait!" This third repetition comes from the sovereign himself.

"You are the squire?"

"Sire?"

"He that was to be hanged for stealing it from the king Arthur?"

"Yes sire, I did steal the sceptre, but not alone."

"No, I suppose that you didn't. And are you telling me that, not only did he steal it from me, he also stole it from Arthur?" The king does sound particularly incredulous.

"I's quite good at stealing," he would have done better to have not spoken at that exact moment.

"That does not speak in thy favour, thieves tend to finish left handed, in these parts." It was the captain of the guard, he that was still pointing his sword at Al's chest.

"Fine, so you stole back the sceptre. Now where is it? And where the devil is my son?"

"Erik? What do you mean? He's not here?" Angelique breaks through the line of guards and rushes up to Galahaut.

"Lady Angelique? What? Why are you here? I heard that there was a mixed party of men and women, but I had no idea that you were with this party."

"Tell me, what has happened to Duke Erik." The anguish
in her voice left, not the slightest doubt of her love for the
noble.

"But that is just it, we don't know. I thought that your
group had kidnapped him and had come to negotiate his
ransom.

" 'Hem, 'hem," the thief seems to something stuck in his
throat.

"Is there something more?"

He looks around in, what can only be described as a
'white fear'. His eyes have dilated, his breath short and
panting. He clenches and unclenches his hands in a
compulsive rhythm.

"Speak!" The king commands.

He crouches down slightly, to be as best protected by the
slight body of the squire.

"I, I knows what's happened to the Duke." And here has
stops, too frightened to continue.

They all wait for a few moments, eager to hear more.

"Speak!" Repeats the captain, agitating his sword, in
Faron's direction.

Faron holds out for a few more seconds, only to finally give in. Another long sigh.

"It's, it's a bit me own fault." There is a wave a reaction from all directions.

"I told someone, and he couldn't hold 'is wheesht, but it weren't really 'is fault. We all knows that silver, spirits and seduction can loosen any man's tongue."

"Who was this traitor?"

" 'E's just an id'yot a clodpate, t'wasn't 'is fault, just plain stupid."

"He sold my son!" The king bellows.

"I, I got's the money. Here." And he throws a heavy cloth bag towards the king.

"Thirty shillin's, thirty pieces o' silver. That's all o' it."

Before anyone can react, Al takes a step forward.

"We'll get him back sire. We'll make it right." Then, as an after-thought, "you can trust us, sire."

"You," his voice softens slightly, "you I feel that I can trust. But him?"

"I will vouch for him, your majesty."

"And I, Lancelot, I will lead the quest to rescue the Duke and win back your love."

The sovereign stops; one can almost hear his slow, steady breathing, a certain sadness might be read on his worn face.

"I have missed my best friend. Find and return my son to me, and your honour will be restored."

The brave knight turns to the common thief, Faron asks Faron, "can you find out where the Duke is being held?"

"I's sure of it."

"You'd better be, or else your own life will be forfeit."

He turns back to the king. "Yeh, I's a good as guessed."

Ch. 42 Dark and Smoky

The tavern is dark and smoky.

The yellow, fatty, tallow candles release thin, grey wisps of dirty, twisting, translucent, tendrils.

That add to the thick, yellow tobacco clouds, of the after-dinner, pipes.

The four men force their way through towards an alcove at the back of the room.

Faron, the thief, is leading the group, he seems to know what he is doing, and where he is going.

Waiting at the table are Michael and Duncan.

Their reactions to the approaching men, are far from identical.

Duncan smiles and jumps up to welcome them; Lancelot and Al he knows from the island.

However. Jay is new to him, but he is just as friendly.

Michael doesn't move.
Michael doesn't even look directly at anyone.
Michael has been a bad boy.
Michael knows that he is about to be punished.
But
Michael is wrong.

"Do you know where he is?" Lancelot has no time for niceties. His only interest is releasing Erik, and restoring his friendship with Galahaut.

"I, I, I thinks so."

"Come." The knight wastes no time, grabs him by the arm, and is ready to drag him out.

"Sire," the other Faron intervenes. "Sire, it late, and we is all tired. Would'st it not be a good idea to stop and make a plan?"

"The plan is to go and liberate the Duke."

"Sire?, Al stops forward, "maybe Faron is right. We would do well to rest and to prepare ourselves."

"That makes sense." Jay, since having come up with the successful plan to free Al, has begun to be looked to as someone to be taken account of.

The knight looks round to the whole group, there seems to be a consensus. He roughly releases Michael and goes to sit down.

251

"Al, go and order drinks, I'm thirsty. And tell the innkeeper that we will require rooms and supper."

Ordering his squire like this, is a means to reinstate his position of authority.

"Now, you, tell me all that you know. Everything!"

Ch. 42 The Interview

The cock had not finished crowing when they arrived at her cottage door.

The air is fresh and bracing, they are stressed and somewhat excited.

The dwelling is small, hemmed in-between similar houses on both sides.

The once white-washed front wall, now greying and streaked.

Some of the other cottages display attention and care for the outside, with well kept and invested gardens, although quite tiny, in front of their miserable homes.

Lancelot bangs, unnecessarily loudly, on the small, pale, wooden door.

He has to repeat this aggressive gesture twice, before a very sleepy and irritated, not so young woman, cracks open the door.

The remains of a heavy coat of white makeup and red lipstick give the impression that she had contracted some awful rare type of skin disease.

She looks up at the powerful knight, surely not having noticed his entourage.

"I only works nights, an' the las' one's not gone yit. You can come back this evenin', I'll make it worth the wait."

And she goes to close the door.

"The services that I need from you will not wait, and have nothing to do with touching your vile body."

A knight is supposed to treat all with kindness and respect, he must be making an important exception for her.

" 'azel, we needs t' talk." Faron pushes his way in front of Lancelot.

"Wha' you doin' 'ere?" Suddenly she realises that there are four men standing on her entrance path.

And not only that, one of them is someone that she knows, and who's helper she has wiled out important information from.

Suddenly she is wide awake, her eyes widen in fear, she tries to slam the door shut in their faces.

She might have been fast enough to block the acrobat, but
knight is another matter.

First, his foot wedges between the door and the frame;
then, with a hefty blow from his shoulder, the door flies
back upon again, sending the woman several feet back
into the room,

"Aaaw," she lands heavily on the old, splintered floor.

The noise has awoken her client, who comes, half dressed
down the narrow stairs to investigate. He takes one look
at the men congregating in her small, front room, and
returns back to the upper floor.

Nobody moves, nobody speaks.

The man, clutching the rest of his affairs, back, scaping
the wall behind, slinks down to the ground floor, gives a
half smile, half nod to the prostate woman on the floor,
and escapes out into the safe exterior.

"Where is the Duke Erik?" He has no patience with this
loose woman.

"D' know."

"Oh yes she does, an' I'll be 'appy to beats it out of 'er."

"Oh no you won't."

"Won't I then?" Faron has a large debt to repay, and she isn't going to be the one to stop him doing it.

" 'E's a knight, 'e's sworn to protect women. 'E can't let you touch me. Can y'a?"

She smiles and drags herself back to her feet.

"Sire," she curtsies, "sir knight, I ask for your protection against this man that thinks to harm me."

"Jus' go back t' the tavern, I'll be joinin' yous in a little minute," Faron smiles in a wicked way.

"No, Faron, she's right. I cannot let you harm her. It is part of my oath as a knight."

"Then, good-day to you gentlemen. Please close the door gently when you leave." She gives Faron a big smile and goes to turn her back on them.

"I am forsworn to protect God and King and all the dwell in their domains. I will not, nor can not accede to any harm coming to this woman, from any of your hands."

She smiles, and gives a small bow of approval to the noble gentleman.

"However, she has implicated herself in the abduction of Duke Erik, the son of King Galahaut, and hence it is my noble duty to arrest her and take her the king for judgement, sentence and punishment."

"Wouldn't that likely be a hanging?" Jay speaks for the first time.

"You, you, you wouldn't?" She half smiles to the knight.

"Madame, I have no choice. As long as the Duke is not returned to his father, safe and sound, you are the only person that can help."

"Of course he would be likely to torture her first, to get out any information that she might have." Jay is clearly enjoying himself here, slightly more so, than can be said for the owner of the house."

"Y' can't, y' can't."

"Sadly, I must. You see, sometimes, being a knight, I have to do unpleasant things." Sighing and shaking his head, he advances towards her.

"I'll tell y', I'll tell y'."

"I thought that you didn't know anything." Lancelot turns to Jay and gives him a stern look. 'Enough is enough'.

"I'll tell everythin' that I know."

"Everythin'," Faron smiles a very evil smile.

Ch. 44 The Rescue

As it turns out, Hazel, not only was implicated in worming out the details of the theft and the handover of the sceptre, but was also the person delivering food to the captive and his jailers.

The idea was simple; first sell the magic stick to Mordred, then, when that was done, find a way to ransom Erik back to his father.

The first part of the mission accomplished, they then had to work out the logistics of the second part.

As one might imagine, these not being professional bandits, and having brought the captive to their own town, to find a way to sell him back to his father, without immediately getting themselves caught, was proving a little complicated to organise.

So, for the moment, they were just keeping him prisoner, until someone could think of something to do.

Lancelot is all for mounting an attack, breaking down the door, and negotiating directly with his sword.

The others are far more cautious, they are concerned that if the kidnappers get scared enough, they could do something stupid, and harm the duke.

Since the morning of the planned execution, Faron has pretty much let the Lancelot personality run everything, like a passenger in someone else's car.

The knight has been driving, Faron has been watching both, the way that he has been handling things, and the eventual outcome.

Although it is obvious that he is brave, strong and determined, unfortunately, our modern man, has noticed, he is not particularly bright.

As has often happened, in his real life, it has been Jay that has found the right things to say, solutions, and, in this incarnation, the strategy to save Al.

Yes, threatening Hazel to take her to Galahaut did get her to talk, but was that really a strategy, or was it also just the truth of what he would do?

Anyway, the others are now busily persuading him to not break the door down, and accept another way to go about the rescue.

Eventually it was the other Faron that came up with a plan that they all could agree to.

"Open up!" He bangs on the door.

" 'oo is it?" A cautious question.

" 'Tis me, Faron, up the door," The door is opened a crack.

"Go 'way, you've naw't t' do 'ere." He goes to close it.

"I've cum t' solve y' problem."

"What problem?"

" 'Ow t' get rid o' the duke."

"What duke?"

"Idyot, I knows all abart it. Michael works f' me. 'E told me abart 'Azel, 'nd he done told me abart your problem. So open the door, an' let us in."

He then opens the door, only to be confronted by the whole group. They are again hidden in the long cloaks and hoods that they wore when fleeing from Camelot.

" 'Oo are these?"

"These is real outlaws, they just escaped from King Arthur." He replies, truthfully.

"An' they'll do the trade with Galahaut?" He sounds honestly relieved.

He lets them into the forest cabin. It is an old hunting lodge, and must have been quite luxurious in its day. The main room is high ceilinged, with a massive fireplace, and generous proportions.

The furniture is all heavy and solid, polished hard wood.

However, the covers and pillows all show signs of much use, and much wear.

There are two other men in the room. All three of them would be in their early to late thirties, bearded, strong and muscular. There clothes are made from strong, spun weave, but are also showing signs of age and wear.

They fit nicely into their surroundings.

They made a start, and reached for their swords when the men entered, but the man that came to the door must be the leader, and when he gestured to sheath their weapons, they immediately obeyed.

"Where is he?" Lancelot speaks for the first time.

"'Es in there." He nods towards a closed door at the far end of the room.

"I trust that he has not been harmed." He continues.

"Naw, 'es worth more alive an' 'elthy."

"Good."

"Right, let's to talkin', what's the deal?"

Lancelot walks to the front door, while Al appears at the door leading to where Erik has been locked up.

Faron can feel the thrill and excitement mounting and filling Lancelot's body.

Yes, he has experienced something similar, often outside a bar or club in the early morning hours.

However, in all those cases, he was either drunk, or stoned, or both.

This surge of adrenaline needs no protective molecules to calm the fear and subdue the protective, survival instinct.

The knight is somewhere, totally aware of the dangers of a fight, but he still relishes the prospect of entering into one.

Fortunately, he is aware that killing these miserable, three men, strong as they might be, would not be worthy of a true knight.

So, if bloodshed could be avoided, it would behove him to calm his inner bloodlust, and find a peaceful solution.

Faron, realising this, heaves a silent inner sigh,

He can feel the reassuring planks behind his back, and smiles.

The smile fails to evoke any sign of relaxation or comfort in the bandit group.

He gently pulls back his cloak, to reveal his long sword, which has already been drawn from its ornate scabbard.

"This is the deal. You walk out of this cabin, without any resistance, or discussion, and I will let you live."

One of the men jumps to his feet, knocking over his chair, and pulls out a long, wicked looking knife.

The leader has not yet made any form of movement, other to scan the room.

Al already has his sword at the ready; Jay has his hand on the hint of his sword, and Faron, street fighter that he is, has a knife, only inches from the back of the second henchman.

It is clear that they would have no chance.

"An' you'll jus' let us go free; no constables, no hunters, no one t' trouble us?"

"If we take the duke, unharmed, and good health, and all the money that you traded the sceptre for, I'll see to it that you come to no harm."

Faron, is having great trouble believing what he is hearing coming out of his own mouth.

Sure there are codes and ethics, but these villains stole the sceptre, sold it and, at the same time, kidnapped Erik with the intent to ransom him off.

If he could converse directly with the man that he was sharing a body with, he would definitely have some searching questions to ask.

The leader goes to get something from his belt.

The four liberators tense, ready to attack.

But there is no need, he throws a heavy, metal key onto the table.

Then, without a word, without another look, pushes back his chair and gets to his feet.

He then, most slowly and deliberately goes to a hook to take down his cloak. If one was to look closely, they might notice that his hand is shaking.

Still not acknowledging the presence of anyone else, he dons his outwear, then turns to a shelf to pick up his sword.

He then unhooks his old leather pocket and places it on the centre of the table.

The others look to Lancelot, who, in response to the unspoken question, moves to the side, and fully opens the door.

They then watch, as he stiffly walks the few feet of the room and exits into the night.

His two subordinates, with much more haste, and much less pride, grab their belongings and rush out after him.

The door is swiftly closed, as once safely secured, they all burst out in peals of laughter.

Seconds later, Jay has grabbed the key and opened the door.

The scared looked young man, takes one look at his saviours, and melts into tears of relief.

Ch. 45 An Unexpected Decision

And so they returned, all was forgiven and even Al, Jay and Faron were allowed to participate to the great feast.

Usually, the 'boys' were only present to serve the invited guests, so this an incredibly unique occasion for them.

Faron, as an acrobat, had also been invited, but in his place, as an entertainer.

From the high table, the real Faron is looking on, looking through the eyes of Sir Lancelot, hero of the hour.

He can feel how troubled the man is, how his look towards Galahaut, his best friend, evokes, … sadness.

It is not easy to read exactly where this sadness is coming from, the link is not that complete.

From the corner of his eye, he perceives Friar Brendan, which produces a strong reaction in the knight's body.

He gets up, slightly startling Galahaut on one side, and Erik on the other.

"Pardon me, I need to confer with the good father," he mumbles, in way of an explanation, as he quickly moves off to intercept the holy man.

"Father, I must speak with you."

"What? Here? Now?" He would much rather stay and benefit from the feast.

"I apologise, but there is something pressing on my mind, and I need someone of confidence to discuss it with."

"Then, please."

"Not here, somewhere quiet." He leads him out to one of the antechambers.

The fat friar sits. He has a large mug of mead that he had in his hands, which he is eying, wondering if it would upset the knight if he would drink some.

"Please, drink, if you must." Yes, he is a little irritated.

He paces the room for some moments, in silence.

"I'm going back to Camelot."

Brendan nearly chokes on his drink.

"Camelot?!"

"Yes, back to Camelot."

"But surely, you cannot be serious. They will imprison you, no they will hang you."

"I have done nothing wrong. Al has explained it all to me. 'Twas the great magician Merlin that has tricked us all. The king Arthur must hear of this."

"He won't listen to you."

"Galahaut is innocent of all wrong-doing. I am also innocent. Merlin is the traitor, and now Mordred has the sceptre, and is likely to attack, as soon as he can mount an army. Arthur must be warned."

"Hmmm," he takes a long, slow drink from his tankard. "I do see your point, but I still doubt that the king will so much as look at you, never mind listen."

"I shall beseech the aid of the queen. Queen Guinevere must believe me."

"Do you believe that she is still in love with you?"

Lancelot stops, Faron is also most interested to find out where he is with this relationship. After all, his own interest still lies with Angelique.

"My feelings for Her Majesty do not enter into this, it is my loyalty for the king which drives me to act."

And, like a twenty-ton stone hammer, it hits Faron on the centre of his deepest, most intimate pain.

'J.J. is again disappointed with me. Yes, we have to go back. Yes, this is the only, the right thing to do. Don't listen to a word that he speaks. He is only here to confuse us, to test us, to lead us wrong.'

The intensity of Faron's reaction finds its way through into Lancelot's psyche.

"It is decided, I will return to Camelot. I will start at first light. Thank you for your counsel. I shall bid all good night. Good night. Oh, and enjoy the rest of the feast."

He turns and is gone.

Ch. 46 Into the Dream

The walls are cold and damp, the rough-cut stones of the donjon prison seem thicker and more imposing now that he is the prisoner and not the master, visiting his condemned squire.

It looks more and more likely that he will be judged in Al's place.

After intercepting him and throwing into this miserable cell, he has been informed that Arthur not only refuses to see him, but has sent messengers to reunite all the other knights of the round table.

The inference is obvious. Arthur wants the agreement of the whole of his banner of knights. And there can only be one agreement that he would be looking for, to revoke his title as knight, and then to hang him as a traitor to the crown

His requests to see the Lady Guinevere, have been treated as some form as ridiculous joke, and frankly all seems rather dire.

'What the fuck was I thinking?' Faron has more than enough opportunity to reflect on the rashness of his impulse to return.

'What interest would either my father or my mother have to hear anything of what I might have to say? They never bothered to listen to me when I was real and alive, here, now, they are king and queen, and I'm the disappointing, adoptive son.'

Lancelot slumps down against the damp wall.

'If there was only some way that I could call for help, maybe, maybe someone might hear me.'

And with that despondent thought they drift into sleep.

Time passes, the sun dips down from the heavens and they have a most wonderful dream.

With the crowing of the cock, comes a solder with breakfast.

No more the thick, meaty broth, exclusively for knights and royalty. A basic meal of bread, cheese and ale, is all that he is served, and for which he would do well to be thankful of.

The day passes particularly slowly.

Faron is feeling more and more; angry, frustrated and depressed.

'Not only did I throw away my freedom in a stupid attempt to sort things out with these people that are not really my parents, but I might still have had a chance with Angelique.

Yes, she was being pretty close with Erik, but Erik is really Duncan, and Duncan can never end up with her.

No story can be written so badly that he would end up with the beautiful heroine.

So, something will surely happen to break up that little, love story.

And if I hadn't been so damn stupid, I would have been there, waiting in the wings, to comfort her in her loss, and then, and then … FUCK!'

He might have even gone so far as to bang his head against the wall, as he once did in his real life.

Fortunately, that is not in the repertory of Lancelot's behaviours.

Finally, the day passes, punctuated with mini-meal breaks, and squatting over the tiny toilet-hole.

He folds down onto the pile of straw and falls into a fitful sleep.

And again he dreams.

He dreams that he is in the banqueting hall, looking up to the royal table.

Strangely enough, not only are, J.J., Maman and Angelique seated there, but also Lancelot.

He looks down at his thin hands and arms, and realises that he is Al.

Al is strumming on a lute, he is about to sing.

Into The Dream

Into the dream
I followed the stream
To the very door
Of your heart
In my innocence

I came to ride
To be by your side
That we came to meet
I'm sure 's
No coincidence

But if you
Part from my sight
Run and hide in -
To the night
Do not part
Break my heart
With indifference

We shared the dream
And followed the stream
To the to open door
Of our love
In our innocence

Nowhere to hide
Here by my side
That we shared a kiss
So pure
With no reticence

And then you
Ran like a deer
You awakened all
Of my fear
That you'd leave
Me to grieve
Your indifference

Into the world
My dream unfurled
As the days they passed
Like our love
Grew my confidence

Then I awoke
Leaving nothing but smoke
You were just a myth
From my sense
Of inconsequence

But that's now all
In the past
'Cus I've found you
At last
You are real
And I feel
That my heart can
Now heal
That sadness
Gives way, to
A new romance

He watches, as he turns, and slowly walks out of the
banqueting hall.

Ch. 47 The Day of the Execution

The last breakfast is a more generous affair; there is also a hunk of cold meat served with the ale, bread and cheese.

Lancelot seems to have little appetite, however, Faron is starving and is ripping it into large chunks and is wolfing it down.

He smiles to himself of just how much, when he really wishes to, he can force the will of the knight to one side.

Which is just as well, as, at that same moment, a priest enters to give him his last rights.

"Have you come to bless me or to gloat at my stupidity?"

"I am sorry, but there is nothing that I can do to help you."

"You seem to be able to come and go as you wish."

"I am a man of the cloth, and," he lowers his tone, "nobody of this castle has any idea of my involvement with your liberating the young man."

"But you helped."

"Only we know that."

"So what happens next?"

"It seems that you will have to go through the rather unpleasant experience of being hanged."

"That's it? That's all the help that you can think to give? 'It seems that you will have to go through the rather unpleasant experience of being hanged'. Thanks, thanks a bunch."

"What more do you think for me to do?"

"Listen, you're the all-powerful guide. You're part of the whole set-up.

Okay, so I sort of screwed up.

Okay, I'll have to go down the snake and start this round again.

Okay, I've got to die.

But, and here's the but, I sure as Hell ain't going to accept that I am to be hanged.

It, it's barbaric, and, and, and, I understand that it takes a long time, and that it's bloody painful."

"I am really, really sorry, but, as I said, there is nothing that I can do. If there was, I would definitely do something to help you out."

He then calls for the jailer to let him out.

"I will be close by, when it is time, and when you might need some spiritual support."

"Fuck-off," and he throws the metal mug at the fleeing friar.

From then on, he doesn't have to wait long before they come to get him.

After several days in the dimness of the cell, the brightness of the day is all but blinding.

In some sort of perverted sense of correctitude, even, would one dare to use the term, 'honour', he is escorted, not by the common guards, but by his peers, the other knights.

The courtyard is more than full, it is completely packed.

The soldiers create a form of human snow plough, or ice breaker and clear a path for him and his 'honour-guard'.

He can soon see the gallows looming above the crowd.

'Fuck, fuck, fuck. Such a fucking, fucking idiot. I had it all and, once again, I've totally succeeded to fuck it up.

If only that dream wasn't a dream, but was real, then it could be okay. Now there's nothing, nor no one that can or will make the smallest effort to get me out of this.'

They arrive at the bottom of the steps. He finds himself being propelled up the creaky boards.

Propelled, but by who?

No, not by the knights, nor the soldiers, not even the executioner.

No, it's that noble fool, Lancelot himself.

Ready to face death with all the courage and dignity of a knight of the round table.

Where Faron would be okay to be carried, kicking and screaming to this ugly, drawn out death, Lancelot is quiet and posed.

"Lancelot, it pains me to have to order the revoking of your title as knight. For your part in the theft of the the Uffington sceptre, and the unlawful liberation of your squire, you are branded as a traitor to the crown and hereby sentenced to death."

Lancelot listens coolly to the condemnation of his king.

Faron is blazing with anger at, yet another unfair criticism, from the fat mouth of his abusive father.

"Do you have any last words?"

Faron is fighting to take control and respond, but, in these last minutes, the noble knight will not relinquish his final act of honour.

"Sire, I did not take part in the theft of the precious sceptre, I did not lie, I cannot.

However, I do now see why it was necessary, and I am fully willing to take complete responsibility for the actions of my squire.

And yes, I did orchestrate the liberation of Al, whom, I consider as a hero, and for that alone I am guilty as charged.

I go to my death with my name and honour intact.

May God have mercy on my soul"

And with that, head high, he directs himself over, towards the noose.

To be, at the same time; quiet, serine and ready to face death, and scared, panicked and totally not ready to face anything, justly describes the inner turmoil happening in the one and the same body.

Faron can feel the rough cord being looped around his throat. The gentle tug as the knot is tightened around his neck.

He closes his eyes, telling himself that this is just some kind of long, drawn-out nightmare.

'It will be unpleasant for a moment, and then I will wake up on the back of Lancelot's horse, and the story will restart.

At least I will know who I am and why I'm here. Or at least, I bloody well hope so.'

Faron is allowing himself to become lost in his reflections of how it will be when he is 'reborn' into this particular existence.

Any second now he will give the signal and the trap will be released.

It will hurt, pain and slow strangulation.

The waiting becomes more and more intolerable.

'Fuck it, just get it over and done with.'

He is about to scream out when it happens.

An explosion erupts overhead.

He jerks his head back, just in time to see the second fork of lighting.

A mighty explosion follows almost immediately.

There is no rain, not even a cloud in the sky.

Something very, very strange is happening.

There is a movement in the crowd. The sound of horses walking forward over the cobbled stones.

The river parts and, not Moses, but Merlin appears, accompanied by no other than Al!

"Wait," the royal magician commands.

Arthur, who's arm has been raised to give the final signal, looks as confused as everyone else.

"The knight has been controlled and manipulated by forces that he has not been able to combat.

In himself, he has been as true a man, as ever there was one.

He, and his squire have been under a powerful spell of no other but Morgan Le Fey, herself.

This is not the first time that she has benefitted from the nobility and innocence of Sir Lancelot to further her evil schemes.

Sire, I beseech you to free this gallant gentleman and restore his rank of knight of the round table."

Faron and Lancelot are equally shocked, surprised and relieved to see and hear that which is happening.

Arthur has neither moved nor spoken for several moments. From out of his shadow, a stately person appears, and gently lowers his arm.

Simultaneously nodding to the executioner to release the noose.

They feel the rope, momentarily tighten, only to be slackened, and finally removed.

Faron, alone, would surely have swooned, only he is sharing this body with a true knight.

Lancelot takes a deep breath, bows to the queen and without another word, nor looking either left, nor right, descends the scaffold stairs and returns to his chambers.

Ch. 48 The Tavern

It is only once safe in their room that Faron can find the space to think.

Not surprisingly, they needed to stop at the 'little room', on their way back.

Fear has an odd side effect of loosening one's bowels.

Now here they are, laying on the soft bed.

Once the fear had passed, it has given place to a deep, deep exhaustion.

'The dream. Of course. But no, it wasn't a dream, it was true, real, fact.'

And. as clear as any memory, he plays back the events of the other night.

He is in the tavern.

A tavern he knows so well.

A tavern where he had spent so many painful nights.

A tavern where he first met Al.

A tavern where Al had spent all his young life.

A tavern that is quite full, the men have finished their day's labour and are rewarding themselves with a well-earned drink.

Safe in the knowledge that their wives are at home, tending the hearth, cooking their supper and putting the children to sleep.

A tavern of happy, rowdy men, where a hooded figure is skulking in a corner, having no idea of what to do.

That he knows that he is wearing something with a hood is due to fact that his vision is partially obscured by something flopping over his eyes.

Which would, to some degree explain why he has failed to notice the corpulent figure that his now seated himself facing him, while he still had time to escape.

This, and that he is focusing on the grain of the wooden table, deeply lost in thought.

"Could I offer a young novice a drink?"

He is about to refuse, when he realises that he recognises the voice.

"Friar Brendan? What are you doing here?"

"I think that first, you might answer me that very same question."

"I, I, I thought that Lancelot might have been mistaken. So I followed him to see what would happen."

"I had the same reflection. And now that you have proven your hypothesis to be just, what do you plan to do."

"…I, I don't know." The despair resonates through his words.

"Well, here, I've bought you a drink, maybe that will help inspire you."

He takes the drink and sips it slowly.

"I'm totally lost."

"Let's think this through," the monk takes a long pull of his own drink.

"Would it be of any value to try and get to see the king?"

"I'm a fugitive, they'd just put me in the same cell as my master, and then hang us together."

"The queen?"

"No chance."

"Then who else?"

"There's nobody else. …Or is there?" The friar stops and waits for the young man to finish his reflection.

"Merlin!"

"Merlin? The magician that orchestrated and manipulated you and Lancelot to steal the sceptre in first place?"

"Merlin also manipulated Arthur. And more than that, if Mordred, which is say, Morgan Le Fey, now has the sceptre, everyone is in danger."

"And you think that he could be convinced to help you and save Lancelot."

"I don't think that he has much choice."

"Well I'll certainly drink to that,"

And they do.

Ch. 49 The Cabin in the Woods

He must have remembered the route from his memories
of Lancelot's visits.

The cabin could well be an enchanted, fairy-tale building,
imagined by a bard, for a story.

It has been constructed of stone and daub, with a heavy
thatched roof. The walls are thickly covered in ivy and
climbing roses.

It is only when one would get close that you could make
it out at all, so well was it camouflaged by combination
of natural colours,

Al takes a deep breath and knocks on the door.

They are clearly equally shocked to see the other.

They might even have simultaneously exclaimed, 'you?',
but they didn't, they just stared, unable to think of what
to say, or to move.

"Who is it?" An old voice inquires from the depths of the
dwelling.

"It's the traitor, you must bind him with a spell and deliver him for execution."

"What traitor?" Merlin gently pushes the young woman to one side, and hobbles through the door.

"You?" Finally, someone managed to voice their surprise.

"Don't let him speak, he might be bewitched. Who knows how he managed to manipulate the others to steal the sceptre from the king."

"Kings, he managed to steal it from two kings." He seems more amused than anything else.

"So why is our 'traitor', appearing here, now, at my doorstep? A doorstep that is usually so difficult to find, that I need to accompany my guests, at least the first time."

"I remember it from the memories of Lancelot, when we were with the Copper Knight."

"And I should know of these things?"

"I believe that you created the Copper Knight, and the magic mirror through which we were sent."

"You do, do you?"

"He knows things of which he should not. He is
definitely bewitched," her golden eyes blazing in anger.

"Calm yourself my dear. He is only a boy, even under a
strong spell, he can do no more than talk,"

"Talking can be dangerous. Taking can turn people's
minds."

"So you wish to talk to me?"

"Yes, sire."

"Come, then let us talk."

"Please, not in there, … not with her."

"You know each other?"

"He is not to be trusted."

"It seems that neither of you trust the other. That said, I
would really like to hear what one, who has stolen
something very dear to me, would put himself into so
much danger, has to say."

"Do not listen to him!"

"Silence! You do not talk to me, so. Now go back about
your business. Come, we shall talk out here. You will
have your interview, alone, here, with me."

They walk away from the house, turning several times on small paths, they come to a small clearing.

There is a heavy, old wooden bench, partly hidden by the overhanging trees behind it.

They sit.

"Now, what particular insanity would make you think that I would be interested in anything that you have to say?"

"F'f'f'first. I, I, I, kn' know, that you created the whole story that g'g'got us to st'st'steal the s's'sceptre."

"The whole story? Eh? You have already mentioned the Copper Knight and the Mirror of Memory. What else do you think that I had my hand in?"

"The, the k'k'kidnapping, the, the whole escape, it w'w'was p'p'planned that I w'w'would read the letter, and the, then escape."

"How interesting."

"I, I, I s'saw you?"

"And how did you see me."

"The, the birds, and, and the bat."

"And how were I birds and a bat?"

"The, the yellow eyes. When a wizard takes over an animal, they have y'y'yellow eyes."

"Very good. And why should I want the sceptre so bad?"

"I, I, f'f'first thought that it was just th'th'that you wanted it for p'p'power."

"And now you don't?"

Al stops speaking, he is trying hard to say something, but he is too scared to proceed.

"Speak boy, what is it that you have to say."

"That, that Morgan Le Fey has tricked you!"

"What?!" The wizard has certainly not been expecting this.

"What the devil are you talking about?"

"Her, Hazel, she is being controlled by her. I saw it just now, her eyes, her eyes were yellow."

"Her eyes are hazel, that is how she has gotten her name."

"She helped kidnap Duke Erik, she helped Morgan to get hold of the sceptre. She has tricked you. She got you to get Lancelot to steal it in the first place.

Her men then tried to steal it from us on the way to Camelot. It was you, the owl that saved us."

"Yes, and that I had the good sense to instruct Faron to follow you back, just in case."

"So you admit it then?"

Now it is Merlin's turn to reflect.

And then, out of totally nowhere he gives a great belly laugh.

"Morgan, Morgan, Morgan, oh you clever, clever, beautiful witch. Yes, yes, you've gotten me here."

Suddenly he gets up to his feet.

"Come, we have work to do."

"Work to do?"

"Why, of course, I'll need to get you some help to steal that damned sceptre a third time."

He is moving much, much quicker than Al would have thought possible.

"Have you gone?" He calls out, as he enters the house.

"Please, please, I know not why I am here." She looks lost and helpless.

"Off you go, m'dear. He's a shilling for your troubles."

"A shilling! A shilling? May God bless y'. You is a kind and gentle man."

"Go on, off with you now." And he gently, but firmly bundles her out.

Al thinks to ask, exactly how she had introduced herself into the magician's house but realises that it might be better not to inquire.

"So you believe me?" He is now having difficultly to accept that this great sorcerer would be able to accede so easily to his own version of reality.

"There is no fool, like an old fool. However, to not allow yourself to see your errors is not foolishness, but stupidity. I can assume to be a fool, but not an idiot."

"So you will help me to free Lancelot?"

"Yes, yes, of course, but since you are here, there is still the question of your ally."

"Sire?"

"Young man, have I not already informed you, that you are to be conferred the task of reacquiring the Uffington sceptre?"

"B'but how?"

"It seems that you are a most resourceful young man. I have the upmost confidence that you will succeed, this third time to retrieve the object."

"What? Alone?"

"But of course not. We are now to help you find an ally that will help you."

"Now? Where?"

"Now? Of course. Where? In what we term as the world below."

"The, the world below?" Fear is making his voice shake.

"Oh, don't be worried. I'm sure that you will feel quite at home there. Come, let us begin."

Ch. 50 The Ally

Al is more than a little concerned about this idea of
Merlin's. He remembers quite vividly how Lancelot
nearly got trapped in another world, when he was helping
the wizard create the sceptre.

"Just relax and listen to my instructions."

'Sure, you stay safety here, while others go into danger to
do your dirty work.' The youth is far from convinced
about the prospect of voyaging to another realm.

"You will find yourself in a place that maybe you know,
maybe you will not." The wise old man begins to explain.

"There you will find a way to go down; it might be an
opening between the roots of a tree, a hole in the ground,
a stairway, a lake, or something else… "

Of course he has heard all this before. He has already
been, with Lancelot to the lower world.

His fear and anguish block the reality of his memories.
Strong emotions can have this effect of taking what we
know, and what we know to be true, and hiding them
from our active consciousness.

"… No matter what it is, it will lead you far, far underground…"

"H'h'how will I get back up?" Al is already starting to panic.

"Don't worry, no one has ever, ever become blocked in the lower world."

"But isn't that what the priests call Hell?"

"Ha, ha," he actually chuckles, "and what do they know of anything? Their beliefs span little more than a thousand years, our truth has been followed for ten times that period."

"But if it isn't Hell, then what is it?"

"If you must refer to a biblical reference, it is much, much more like their Garden of Eden."

"Garden of Eden?"

"Yes, every-one and every thing are there to help and support you. And not only that, all the animals, trees and other beings can communicate with you."

"Other beings?"

"Yes, you know, fairies, elves, tree sprites, that sort of stuff."

"If everything is so kind and friendly, then why are you not going yourself?"

"Because," he smiles gently at Al, "because I already have a fistful of allies. Have you never heard of a witches' familiar?"

"It's a magical cat?"

"It's an ally from the world below. As is my owl, and other friends. Some you are able to see, some, not."

"Oh," so he had been there, himself, before.

"Once you arrive in that other world …"

"If it's like the Garden of Eden, then there would be sky for the birds to fly in and water for the fishes."

"Exactly, because it is a world below our own, doesn't mean that it is in some sort of cavern. Not at all, it is a world as this one, with sky and land and oceans and lakes."

"Alright then. So, when I arrive there?"

"You will be met by something. Most likely an animal. It might be your first ally, or it might just be a messenger to take you to him."

"Him?"

"Or her. You will do as you are asked, you will listen if there is information for you. When the sound of my drum changes its rhythm, you will return to your place of arrival and will then return up to the spot of the beginning of this journey."

"How?"

"You will know when it happens. Lie down, your talking tires me. We shall begin."

And with that, he takes up his little drum and begins to beat a slow rhythm.

Al lies down and allows his eyes to close and his mind to drift.

To begin with he is invaded by thoughts and ideas and convinced that this magic voyage would never work.

And then, he finds himself walking along the coast of Sorelais. The wind, as often, is quite strong, blowing is hair in front of his eyes, temporarily blinding him from time to time.

He looks round and notices a path leading down to the sea. Climbing over the rocks, he sees that there is an almost circular gap created by a number of big stones.

'Okay, let's find out what this all about,' and he lets himself drop into its centre.

He has braced himself to fall at speed, only, he doesn't.

In fact, he finds himself floating gently down, and down, and down, and down.

'Curiouser, and curiouser,' the words resound in his head, without any understanding of why he should think of them.

Poof, he softly lands in a pile of leaves. He is at the entrance of a type of cave.

He gets to his feet and wonders out into the woods outside.

'So, who is here to welcome me?' He is starting to think that he will be on his own, when he hears a light stomping coming from the ground to his left.

And there it is, a little, fluffy rabbit. Impatiently stamping its foot, waiting to be noticed by the big, stupid human. (Or at least that is how Al is reading the situation).

"Okay, what's next?" In answer to the question, the small animal turns and runs off.

Al has a hard time keeping up with him.

Out of breath, he is starting to worry that he will lose his guide before arriving at the destination, where-ever that might be.

It runs into a clearing and then suddenly stops.

Before Al has the chance to catch his breath, a large, red fox pounces on the rabbit and wrestles it to the ground.

'So much for love and friendship to all,' he bitterly reflects.

The feline lets the poor creature drop and trots over to the human.

"So, what have you learned so far?"

"That I can't run as fast as a rabbit, and that no matter how fast you might run, someone is always going to get you in the end," he responds bitterly.

"A fox can run faster than a rabbit, and what you see is not always what is really happening."

"What do you mean?"

"You believe that the rabbit passed through here by accident, that I arrived unexpectedly and for that he is now dead?"

"Pretty much."

"Pretty wrong."

"How's that?"

" 'Cus I ain't dead!" The rabbit jumps up, laughing at the startled look of the young man.

"What?"

"First lesson of being a fox…"

"…Being a fox?"

"I'm talking now, shut up and listen, and maybe, just maybe you might learn something."

"Please don't int'rupt, the teacher is teachin'." The dead rabbit is enjoying himself.

"The first lesson of being a fox is think more than the other guy.

Most people, humans included, react most of the time emotionally.

They don't think that they do, but most of the time, their actions are motivated by their feelings, the mind only finds reasons and excuses to explain them."

Al is feeling rather lost. He looks to the only other, from which he can get any feedback.

"The teacher, 'e is teachin'."

"Second lesson, let them think that they know better than you.

Arrogance is the number one killer, of any creature, in any world.

Once they have decided that they are in control, that is the moment that you have them."

Al finds a soft, moss covered rock and sits himself down. This crazy fox is saying some really weird stuff, but, but maybe not so very crazy, after all.

"He who talks least, hears the most.

This is soooo obvious, yet so few people take any notice of this.

Next; it is easier to feign weakness than the feign strength.

An adversary will quicker believe that they are stronger than you, it panders to their egos."

Yes, he is saying interesting things, 'must try and remember these'.

"Never underestimate your enemy but try to get them to underestimate you.

Always imagine that your enemy is much, much cleverer than they seem, they might have a teacher as rusé as I am."

Al is starting to enjoy this training session.

"Take your time to plan and learn to wait. It is only in the moment of action that speed is important.

Thinking up a strategy can and should take time. When a situation is difficult or complex, it pays to think through all the possibilities. Otherwise you will find yourself outfoxed."

"Something that never happens to you."

"No, it has happened to me." He turns and shows a nasty scar running down one side of his back.

"I hope that you won't have to learn through your own painful experience, as I did."

"Sorry. Please continue."

"That's it. That's all the serious stuff."

"And now?"

"And now you will learn how to run. How to run, like a fox."

Al shrugs his shoulders, lost.

"Come, let's run." Al gets up but finds that his front half is heavier than he remembers and is now moving on all fours.

He feels, that which were his arms, are now perfectly positioned to take his weight and balance his movement, while his back feet punch into the ground, lift and propel him forward.

The closest experience that he has had that comes to mind is swimming, although that movement was both arms and legs in unison. Here there is a definite separation between the front and the back appendages.

This is totally exhilarating. He can feel the powerful, pulsating propulsion of arms and legs, as if he were galloping.

Yes, that is it, it is a form of gallop, but being the animal, not a rider, is fundamentally different. A rider feels the power of the horse, here there is no separation, he is movement, he is the flow, he is the power.

And yet, not only that. There is also the awareness; he knows where he is, where he is going, where to place his feet, (even at this speed), what is in front, animals, plants, everything.

His eyes, ears and nostrils are functioning at a level of sensitivity that he could only image possible.

At this speed it is totally impossible to differentiate what or which sense is perceiving what.

He just knows; at such a rate that it is experiencing the inputs, that he can only relate to them as a sort of intuition.

Finally, the fox slows down.

He notices a beat, the drum, it has changed its rhythm.

"Come, we will return you to your world."

"Will I ever meet you again?"

"Only if you call."

They have arrived back at the mouth of the cave like structure.

He turns to ask what the fox means, but is too late, it has already departed.

Al wants to go back to find him but finds himself being gently sucked upwards.

After a much shorter time, he is again back on the shore and almost immediately back on the bed of … straw in the cold, damp donjon cell of the castle.

Ch. 51 Council of War

To be once more in the presence of the king, was not going to be comfortable for any of them.

Lancelot cannot position himself between his want and need to be, once more accepted by his king and adoptive father, and his blazing anger to have been, not only refused to be heard, but all but hanged for his trouble.

Faron is also fuming against the continual disacknowledgment visited on him by his father.

On the other side; whether or not, he was truly under the influence of Morgan Le Fey, or not, the father in question, is still showing a poorly covered up fury against the knight.

Al is also present, as is the wily Merlin.

"Sire, your honours and titles have been restored, but not your welcome in my house."

"Then I should beg your leave, and thank you for your benevolence in letting me leave, alive." Faron can feel the rage, boiling in the knight's body, if only there was some way to be able to express it more directly.

However, he is conscious that this choice of words is still a polite and indirect attack on this, all-powerful monarch.

"Then God's speed. And please to take you're squire with you."

"Again, I think your highness for his bounty." He mimics a bow and turns to leave.

"Before you both depart, I will desire to exchange a word with your young man."

Lancelot hesitates a moment before agreeing to allow his squire to spend even another minute with this manipulating magician, even if he did, finally, save his life.

"As you so wish."

He turns to Al, "I will be waiting for you at the stables, do not keep me waiting long."

Of course, the message is meant for Merlin, but it has to be passed in this fashion.

As they turn to leave, Faron has a huge feeling of frustration to not be able to be present at this meeting between Al and the old rogue.

They bow and all go to leave.

As they are passing the doorway, Faron experiences a peculiar sensation. He turns his head, only to see Lancelot descending the stairs.

"Come," he then turns to follow Merlin towards his own chambers.

They enter the heated, heavily tapestried room, and he watches as the sage makes some strange movements with his arms, muttering under his breath,

"There, now we shall not be overheard. Come, sit."

He gestures towards one of the comfortable chairs, set facing the roaring fire.

So he sits as instructed, and waits to hear as to why he is here.

"You know that Mordred has acquired the sceptre, and has surely given it to his God mother, his aunt, Morgan Le Fey?"

He silently nods his head.

"It will be guarded both by magic and by normal guards."

Again, he nods.

"I sent you to the lower world to find your power animal, an ally, which you did."

"Yes."

"You are the only person that I trust that could steal back the sceptre."

"What? No!" And yet, this is not the first time that he is hearing this information. He heard it that night in Merlin's little house.

Yes, it might have seemed like a dream, at the time, but he knows that it wasn't.

Maybe he didn't react then, as he was most focused on getting to Camelot and saving Lancelot from being hanged, but Merlin had informed him of his plan.

"You know that this is your destiny."

Al does not know that this is destiny and is about to make this abundantly clear to Merlin.

Unfortunately for him, Faron realises that this must surely be part of his challenge in this world. To go where no man has gone before, this is the voyage of the small squire Alain.

He smiles at his own joke.

"Why do you smile?"

"It is my destiny." He almost says 'density', but he is not George Mc Fly, and this is another fantasy, altogether.

"Then you will undertake this quest?" A third reference crosses his mind.

"Yes, I will take this impossible mission." He can feel the fear and resistance coming from the body itself.

Al is totally terrified, his heart is beating, fit to pop, but Faron is fully in charge.

What has happened that has given him so much control of the person, at this time, is a question to ponder on, at a later moment.

All that matters, is that now, here, he has total control, and he has agreed to go and steal the magical sceptre for the third time. Only now, it is the witch, Morgan Le Fey that has it, and she must be well aware that someone, soon, will be trying to get their hands on it.

"We will be all counting on you."

"I'll not let you down, I'll not let anyone down."

Feeling ten-foot-high and ready to eat a dragon, Faron marches Al out of the room, down to the stables and over to Lancelot.

"I won't be coming with you, I'm going to steal the Uffington sceptre, again."

"Do you know what you're doing?"

"Piece of cake." Al gets onto his little horse, and leaving Lancelot looking more than a little nonplussed, rides off into the quiet countryside.

Could he be whistling the theme song of a well-known science-fiction series?

Ch. 52 The Lonesome Trail

He makes his way inland and picks up the Roman road from Exeter to High Cross.

He hasn't stopped to count the money that Merlin had thought to finance his journey with, but it felt cheerfully heavy, jingling in the solid, leather pocket, safely attached to his belt.

From High Cross he had the choice to either return along the road towards Chester and then Manchester, or to stay on the Fosse Way and take the Eastern route to Lincoln and then join Ermine Street and carry on up to York.

Not wishing to take the risk to run into Lancelot or Galahaut, he chooses the more Eastern path.

Along the way he has not spoken to anyone.

Before entering an inn or tavern, he dons his hooded cape, exchanges a few words about his needs to the innkeeper, and then installs himself into any quiet corner or alcove that he can find.

However, he has, just the same, acquired a travelling companion.

On one of his first stopping breaks, he was sitting
finishing off his bread and soup, when he noticed a
commotion in the room.

The fellow diners and travellers were laughing and
throwing assorted objects at something that was weaving
in and out of the tables and chairs.

Finally, the little rat, as that is what it was, made its way
under Al's table.

The men, not being able to get a good target and not
wanting to upset the young monk, decided to leave it be,
and carry on with other forms of amusement.

Having nothing better to do, the supposed novice monk,
dropped several pieces of bread down to the shaking
rodent. Before taking himself off to bed.

On the way up, he fancied that the tiny spider, hanging
from the rafters had shiny, yellow eyes. The idea made
him smile.

The next morning, he breakfasted in the very same
corner. And much to his surprise, the rat appeared on the
table, walking boldly up to his plate.

Blatantly waiting for and expecting to be fed.

Al placed a piece of biscuit on the palm of his hand and
waiting to see what would happen. The rat advanced
several steps towards him before stopping and sniffing,

It seemed that it was about to renounce the offer, when, unexpectedly, it relaxed and climbed onto his hand and took the food.

Then, it ran off back onto the table and gulped down the crumbly snack.

'Okay, but will you dare a second time?'

So, he breaks another portion off the whole and places that onto his hand.

This time there is hardly any hesitation.

The third time, the rat doesn't even bother to leave his hand before eating.

By the time that the meal was finished, the two had come to an understanding, and the rat allowed itself to be picked up and dropped into the dark warmth of the inside of his rough jerkin.

Al smiled at the spider and left to continue his journey.

Along the road he would often notice a stray bird, sometimes a kestrel, a lady-hawk, a peregrine falcon.

While inside, there might be a yellow-eyed, cat, dog, mouse, or maybe even a spider.

He is sure that he is being spied upon, but it is of no matter, all is well. If anything, it is re-assuring.

However, his journey was not without incident.

On the third morning out from Camelot, his breakfast was interrupted by the stable boy, all a-panic.

"Sire, sire, your horse, I've no idea how it could have happened, it wasn't my fault."

Al's heart begins to pump in machine-gun bursts.

"My horse, my horse, what has happened to him?"

"It wasn't my fault."

"What has happened to my horse? Is it hurt?" That would really be a disaster.

"Someone must have badly closed the door of the box, it must have gotten open."

"He has run off?"

"We can't find him."

At that moment the innkeeper arrives.

"We are so very sorry. We have already sent men off to find your horse, I'm sure no ill will happen to her. And, and, while we are recovering your horse, everything is on the house; food, drink, room, everything."

"In that case, since I cannot leave, please ask the maid to make up a big fire in my room, and bring up a bath,"

A pretty little starling entered through the open door and was perched on the table, pecking happily at the few crumbs that were left lying there.

"Please let me know as soon as you find my horse."

"Just as soon as we do," the owner assures him.

'Odd coincidence that it is my horse that had its box badly closed', he reflects on heading back up the rickety stairs.

The horse, suitably exhausted, and of no use for the rest of the day, was returned by mid-afternoon,

The other happening was at the Parish of Winteringham, between Lincoln and York, where one would take the ferry to traverse the Humber.

He had already crossed Mordred's army, they were camped at Bracebridge Heath, at the point where the Fosse Way joins Ermine Street just outside Lincoln.

It spread out across a great number of fields.

Al had never seen an army, but then, for that matter, neither had Faron.

So, it was impossible to know which of the two souls was most impressed, or most scared.

However, the magical sceptre was not to be found here.

The Lady Morgan Le Fey, was camped at Catterick, which is just south of the market town of Derlinton, and forty-two miles north of York.

For some unknown reason, the ferry was not running that very day as there was problem with the boat.

Another lazy day, another lost day for no clear reason.

Once past York, Al wasn't long to meet up with the small army unit protecting that most precious of objects.

Just a boy and his rat against a whole army unit, now that is going to be an interesting challenge.

Ch. 53 Three for Three?

The night was more than chilly, but the shivers are more fear and excitement than cold.

England is a country were having a totally clear, cloud-free night is often more the exception than the rule.

Tonight, was no exception, although the night is dry, there is, just the same, a healthy blanket of clouds, reflecting a sad, grey mantle above.

'Excellent,' he smiles, 'just the perfect weather to go thieving.'.

The army unit, although not huge, has, just the same, about twenty tents in all.

The soldiers, not expecting any form of attack seem calm and relaxed. Most of them are squatted on blankets around one of the many fires that are dotted around the camp.

They will, more than likely have just finished eating, now happily chatting and drinking.

'Like a fox, like a fox,' he skulks down into the shadows. Silently weaving his way towards the centre of the encampment. Surely, she will have her marquis in the most protected area possible.

Has he called his ally? Has he joined with him? Or is he just finding his own inner fox?

Who knows? Only there is something very fox like about Al this night.

On several occasions, soldiers pass, but he has heard them coming from long before, and has had, more than enough time to secrete himself into some dark corner, or other.

With his heightened senses, they all seem particularly slow and heavy, that, and very, very smelly.

'This is too easy,' again he smiles to himself.

The witch, princess, has an oversized, ornate tent. He can see her shadow moving around inside. Now she has stopped, the figure shortens, she must be sitting.

He will have to wait, there is no point rushing.

And so he folds himself into a dark corner of one of the facing tents, and settles himself, for as long as it takes.

An owl flies overhead, but it doesn't stop.

'Good evening, enjoy your flight,' he mumbles to himself.

Not much later, the figure stands up and moves around the tent. Then, the flap opens and the majestic figure steps out.

Although he cannot see her face, he can easily hear her reminding the two guards to keep their eyes peeled, the precious sceptre will guarantee them victory.

As soon as she has moved away, he steals over to the back of the canvas dwelling and cuts a small hole in the side.

It is just big enough for him to crawl through but would not be noticeable in the dark for anyone passing.

Once inside, he is impressed to see the comfort of this temporary home.

The floor is covered with skins, there is a decent sized bed, a table, around which are several chairs, and, facing away from him, a large throne.

He breathes a short sigh and is about to start searching for the magical rod, when a voice comes from the ornate, regal chair.

Although it is not possible to see who is sitting on it, there is no mistake as to who it is.

"Congratulations, to have gotten this far, is quite an accomplishment." She gets up and glides over to him.

"In fact, I am most impressed."

Al does not respond.

"Please, sit, we should talk."

There are some chairs facing the throne, Al goes to sit, he has an air perplexed.

"You are but a humble squire." He vaguely nods his head.

"Yet you can both read and write." Another nod.

"It was you that helped Lancelot climb out of his morbid life-style, after he was thrown out by both Arthur and the queen.

And you have been helping him and supporting him ever since."

"I do what I can."

"You almost got yourself hanged stealing the sceptre the second time, and yet you went to Merlin to help save him, after he was recaptured by Arthur."

"He helped save me the first time."

"He and a group of others."

"How do you know all this?"

"I know many things, knowledge is power."

Faron smiles to himself, how many times has this dictum been heard throughout history?

"Then you will know that Lancelot is a true knight."

"Yes, and you are a true squire."

"I take that as a compliment."

"I take you for a fool." Although the words are hard, her tone is soft, she sadly shakes her head.

"I don't understand."

"But you do. Life has not offered you a position commiserate with your capacities."

Although Al does not understand the word, as Faron does, the sense of the phrase is clearly comprehended.

"And what should I be in life?" He is, if anything, intrigued with this conversation, it certainly wasn't what he had intended to happen.

"You should be a personal advisor."

Even Faron is not clear on her meaning.

"You should have the power and authority and comfort that someone as brave and cunning and intelligent as you should have."

"Are you offering me a job?" Faron can not help himself but react.

"That is not a term that I would think to use, but, if you wish to use such a term, then yes, I am offering you job.

A very good job, a job where the person that you are, and the things that you can do, will bring you the respect that you seek.

You; who have been rejected by your real parents, brought up in the most miserable way, who has fought, with every ounce of his will to better himself, in every way conceivable.

And what can you possibly expect from life? To be well treated? To be well treated as a slave?

Lancelot would have left you to rot and die on the rope, if the others would not have pushed him to act.

Remember how he was when he left your prison that night. He wasn't going to do anything to help you."

"How can you know that?"

"Because I was there. I wanted to see, to hear, to know. I too needed to understand why you, a simple squire, had chosen to risk his own life, to steal the sceptre from Arthur."

"And you understand now?"

"Yes, yes, I believe that I do. You are looking to find your own pride, your own self-esteem, your self-respect."

Faron is totally taken, how can she know of his real mission on this fake world?

"And working for you will bring me all of these things?" Al questions the powerful princess.

"I will guarantee it," she smiles down at him, it seems that he is softening to her arguments.

"And betraying everyone will bring me self-esteem?"

"They have all betrayed you … They will never treat you any better than the slave that you are to them.

Not even the princess Angelique, whom you love, but to her, you are as insignificant as a well-loved … horse."

"And you would not betray me?"

"I am offering you the opportunity to break from your serfdom, to become a free-man. No-one has ever offered you as much."

Al smiles, then gently takes to his feet.

"I have heard that the path to Hell is paved with good intentions. I thank you for the good intent that you have towards me, but it cannot be my path.

I was willing to die to protect those that I care about, nothing has changed for me since then."

She also gets up, smiles, sadly to herself and goes to open the tent flap.

"You and you, come and tie him up. You, bring my cloak back."

Two soldiers enter, bringing in a bundle of cord. There follows a woman, of equal height and shape as the princess who takes off the expensive outer-garment and goes to hang it on a hanger from a wardrobe hidden behind a curtain.

The soldiers grab Al, who, in no way resists, and back him against the heavy, central tent-pole. They then proceed to bind his hands behind him.

What they do not notice, is that while they are holding his arms, Al turns his hands so that the palms are facing outwards.

As they loop the cord around his wrists, he presses the backs of his hands together, slightly forcing his wrists apart.

This applied pressure allows the soldiers to assure themselves that the rope is firmly tied and that there is no means for him to release himself.

In truth, he has created a half an inch of play in the cord, a half inch that is all the difference between being a predator or bring prey.

The soldiers and the woman are dismissed.

"Are you still so sure that you wish to refuse my generous offer?"

"Don't worry, you know that I am not alone."

"Quite the contrary, I am assured that you are."

"Yes?"

Since you have been to see Merlin, I have personally followed you every step of your journey."

"The birds? The dogs? The cats? The Mice?"

"Even the spiders."

"Oh."

"So, I am sure that you have spoken to no-one during the whole of this journey. However, Merlin might have contacted people and organised them to meet you."

"Yes, yes he would have."

"Which is why I organised for your horse to escape and for the ferry to be blocked.

Being two days behind schedule, and with no way to contact you, if there were people waiting for you, they would have presumed that, for some reason or other, you would not be arriving.

Which is why I am more than certain that you, young man, are totally and utterly alone in this ridiculous endeavour."

"Why ridiculous?"

"Because it was deemed to failure from the beginning. And which, sadly, since you refuse to accept my very generous offer, I will be forced, as an example to others, to have you executed."

"It won't be the first time that someone had thought to have me executed."

"But it will certainly be the last."

Al stops for a moment before answering.

"Your Majesty?"

"What?"

"You know, even having stolen it twice, I have never seen the sceptre close up. Would it be too much to ask, before you have me executed, and since I am safely tied up here, to allow me to see it once, close up, before I die."

"You are such a strange little rat, …, but then again, what harm can it do?"

She disappears behind a screen, and one can just make out certain sounds and the flashes of colour and the smell of burning.

"Here, feast your eyes of the cause of your demise."

"You could bring the … reason for my death, just a little closer."

Not being totally confident, she first circles the post to confirm that he is, indeed, tightly bound.

As soon as she has passed, he twists his palms together, releasing the extra tension on the thin rope.

It only takes another second to slip his hands out from his bonds.

He carefully catches the cord, so it doesn't fall to the floor.

She approaches with the intricately woven, glowing staff.

"It's quite ironic that this will be the last thing that you see ever."

"Actually, it's the last thing that you will see for quite a moment, yourself."

"What?"

"NOW!"

Several things happen in much the same time.

The rat jumps out of his tunic, its fiery, golden- yellow eyes filling her view.

Hurling itself towards her face, she shrieks and moves to protect her eyes with both hands.

There is a loud ripping sound, that comes from the roof of the tent.

This is the moment that Al has been waiting for.

He lunges out, arms outstretched.

The sceptre drops but does reach the floor.

Someone drops from the roof and does reach the floor.

The moment that Al has it in his hands, the rat squeaks and there is strong wind that passes through the tent, extinguishing all the lanterns.

However, there is no light to be seen from outside either, only the sounds of the soldiers cursing the sudden, intense wind and rain that has drenched them, their fires and all the lights.

A second body drops through the rented canvas.

The first has already gotten to his feet and has pinned her arms to the side of her body.

His accomplice, quickly rises up and tightly gags the struggling witch.

A pile of clothes drop from the gap.

Al slips out of his clothes and dons the uniform.

Now it is the turn of the princess to be tied up, attached to the pole.

Unfortunately, being a real witch, she has never learned the escapologist trick of turning her hands inwards, to facilitate escaping.

A rope, with a series of loops is lowered down.

Faron takes the sceptre, wraps it up in a heavy cloth and places it in a quiver, which he slings over his shoulder.

Al grabs the rope ladder and, with help from the other two, climbs up to the roof of the tent.

A helpful hand reaches down to drag him up and onto the stretched canvas.

The other two easily climb back up and out.

There are three cords stretched out into the darkness. The young man notices that there is a triangle structure lashed onto the central post, sticking up out of the tent.

Attached to each of the corners is one of the ropes, two at the bottom, a third at the apex.

They help him into a type of harness also made out of knotted cord. There are three loose ends trailing out of the contraption.

One is looped over the cord at the top, and tied in a loose hoop. The others are much longer, one of the men starts to edge himself across the tightropes holding onto one of the hanging ropes.

He is quickly enveloped into the heavy darkness. After the night being relatively clear, there is now a thick bank of heavy cloud covering the sky.

There is much commotion below, as the soldiers attempt to relight their torches, unfortunately with little success, each try fails due to a strong, unexpected gust of wind.

After several long moments, there are some sharp tugs on the rope. Al takes to the ropes and edges his way forward.

The darkness underfoot does little to give a feeling of safety, which is why the harness and the guide ropes have been put into place.

He steps slowly and carefully one foot after the other.

Unfortunately, the strong, light impeding winds also affect him here, on his temporary swing.

He grabs hold of the third rope to regain his balance.

"Down, down," shouts one of the conspirators. He crouches down, limiting the possible arc and lowering his centre of gravity.

A few seconds and the swaying diminishes, his heart slows and his breathing calms.

And then; several paces further, the silhouette of another and bigger tent looms out of the darkness.

The same triangular apparatus is tied to one of the tent posts, and there is another rope ladder hanging down the side.

He is quickly helped out of the harness, and he then quietly descends the ladder.

It is only a few moments more before they are all four strolling through the camp.

And then … freedom. …

Ch. 54 Up and Down

To avoid any chance of being captured, they have first
pointed themselves North,

From there on they took to the West.

They had galloped, walked and galloped until the horses
could go no further, and then camped in the little woods
not far off of the main thoroughfare.

It was only after passing Penrith and joining the
Manchester road that the fear of getting caught began to
release itself, and Faron could take the time to appreciate
his magnificent coup.

He had left Merlin and Camelot with nothing other than
the intention to find and restore the sceptre to its rightful
owner, that being Galahaut.

On arriving at the first hostel, he felt the need to keep a
low profile, not knowing if there would be any spies
watching him.

It was then that he noticed the first of the many yellow
eyed creatures.

Was it Merlin, or was it Morgan Le Fey?

No way, at this time to be sure, but if it was the wizard, maybe he would not have stayed hidden away, as a muddy-brown mouse.

Going up to his bedroom, he suddenly began to feel very alone in this, more than difficult, 'mission impossible'.

What he would really need would be a team of experts to help him construct a magnificent sting.

Merlin was clearly incapable to do anything useful while Morgan has the sceptre.

Lancelot could be counted on to head a direct charge, but anything more subtle would be a little beyond his strengths.

Not to discount his firm decision to no longer interfere in this affair.

And so he goes to sleep, vaguely wishing to find those that could help…

"Wake up y' sloomy 'ead, it's y' turn to buy."

Faron opens his eyes, only to shut them immediately to block out the acrid pipe smoke that burns his pupils.

Gingerly, he opens them again.

Some detailed dream he is having.

The sights, sounds, smells and smokiness of the tavern are almost over empowering.

"What?"

"You done fell asleep. It's you that's payin'." Michael?

"If you's tired, maybe you should go t' bed." And Duncan.

"Na' 'e jus' don't wants to pay."

"He, here's a groat go'on get the drinks," He fishes into his old leather pocket and pulls out a big, worn, tarnished, silver coin. Which he throws, not so gently, towards Michael.

"Ta, Faron." He takes the trophy and disappears to get more drinks.

'Faron? Of course, Faron, who else would I be? Who else can help me, if I can't even help myself?'

Somehow, even if it is only a dream, the idea that he, as Faron, might be able to do something to help himself, this, to Al, feels right.

He waits until Michael returns with the drinks.

"We's a job to do."

"How's that?" Duncan questions his boss.

" 'Tis well paid?" Michael only asks the important questions.

"We'll be surely well paid. We start's first thing in the mornin'."

"What's the job?"

"Can't say f' now, you'll be knowin' when y' needs to know."

"Well paid? Promise."

"Would I lie t' you?"

"Just drink up, if we're to start early, we's needs to go t' bed." Duncan finishes his sermon and picks up his drink.

Faron woke up the next morning, puzzled, Was it just a dream, or did he really find himself in the body of 'The Faron', The Faron of the Faron Show?

As there was no way to confirm or infirm his question, he contented himself with thinking up a plan, in which the three acrobats could well participate.

During the day he noticed, on several occasions that there was a lone bird, often a bird of prey, that would pass, relatively close, and then fly off.

That evening, he met up with the rat, but thought little of it.

He did notice, however, the shiny, yellow eyes of the spider, as he mounted the stairs.

Once alone and in bed, he relaxed and thought about how it felt last night, in his dream of being Faron.

Gently, he felt some form of subtle shift, and once again he was aware of the heavier and rougher body and energy.

They are sitting around a small camp fire. They have finished eating and are enjoying a late smoke before turning in.

"But what's the plan?" Duncan is sounding concerned, he likes to know as much as possible before he commits himself.

"And who is we goin' to sell it to, this time?"

"Listen, I will tell y' when it's time."

"I don't think that y' know nothin'."

"I knows 'ow to give ya a good whoppin', now you stop doggin' me and finish y' pipe. We've a good ways t' go t'morrow."

Faron can feel the stress and tension of having to keep his little troop in order, without having the slightest idea of what he is supposed to be doing.

So he settles the older man against a tree and allowing him to relax with the smoke and nicotine of the pipe, to reflect on the plan that he has thought up.

It is a very foxy plan.

Faron pulls at his pipe, dreams into the trick, and smiles in amusement.

The next morning, he is totally convinced that he can transfer his consciousness not only into Lancelot and Al, but now, also into 'The Faron', as he has chosen to name his other self.

Being in such a good mood, he is happy enough to meet up again with the rat, at the breakfast table.

However, it is only when the tiny rodent is in his hand, only inches from his face, that the eyes change colour, from deep brown, to bright yellow.

'Merlin, the cheeky little magician.

Now, if you are the rat, that means that all the other yellow eyed creatures must all be controlled by the witch.

If she has been watching me all this time, then she must know that I've not spoken to anyone since I've left Camelot.

She will be expecting me to be doing this alone.

Well, I'll not be doing this by myself, but with myself.'

And he set out on the next leg of the journey, feeling, for the first time, in a very long time, that something might just work itself out.

He spent quite a lot of that day's journey, trying to remember all the science-fiction and fantasy novels and films that he could, where the hero can jump from body to body or place to place.

Although he could vaguely remember having seen or read quite a few, the only one that he could place definitively was the guy from, 'Pawns of Null-A' that could register a location and then, at will, materialise there, whenever he would wish.

And so, he began to experiment with the idea of being able to move between the two bodies, without having to fall asleep.

As there was little else to occupy his mind during the long day's ride, he had ample time to work on this.

Until, with an increasing ease, he began to succeed to jump from Al's body, into that of Faron, and back again.

Which is how, on that fateful night, he was able to orchestrate the entrance of the acrobats at exactly the perfect moment to disable and tie up the Wicked Witch of the North.

So now they were descending from the North towards the known roads that would lead them to the safety and security of the Isle of Man, or Sorelais, as Galahaut's island is still called.

Only, of course, it doesn't.

Ch. 55 Another Choice

He is focusing on a slightly tricky bit of path. There has been quite some rain and going downhill is rather slippery.

He is taking his time, choosing that strategy, rather than risk finding himself falling into a river of mud.

From out of nowhere, he feels himself being dragged backwards.

His first thought is that he was about to slip, and one of the others has caught him and is stopping him tippling head over heels, over the horse's head.

Only, the sensation of being drawn is that of his whole being, not just his shirt or breeches.

A split second later and he recognises this as the sensation when he splits from one body and jumps into the other.

Only Al and Faron are both here, and he has not intentionally chosen to travel between the two.

"I'll not hear any more on this!"

"Sire, it is of no sense." He recognises Galahaut, he is back the King's castle.

"Erik will not endanger himself." He, Lancelot is bellowing.

"I will do as I wish. You have no rights over me." Erik is also shouting.

"But I do, m'lad, and I forbid it."

"Father, please, I must." He responds to the king's injunction.

"It is suicide," Lancelot is attempting to convince them both.

"And exactly why, my heart brother, would you be choosing to take this fools quest?" Galahaut is doing his own best to keep a level tone and level head.

"It is my right, it is my choice, it is my responsibility."

"Only days ago, you arrived vowing to never bother if Arthur nor Guinevere were alive or dead."

"This is not only about them."

"It is also about the Lady Angelique," Erik is eloquent in his anguish for the safety of this young woman."

"So you wish to risk your life to try and save the life of this noble lady?"

"If I do not undertake this, then you will not have the means to hold him here," Lancelot glances at Galahaut's hot headed son.

"You would do this to protect my son?"

Lancelot stops and ponders his answer.

"It would sound as the most noble of acts. And truly, it is one strong reason to girdle my sword-belt, one more time.

… But it would not be the whole of the truth.

I cannot bear to stand on the side and see the king Arthur slaughtered in a vile trap. He took me in and draw me to him, he kissed my brow and designated me as his son."

"But he exiled you, twice."

"And was about to have you killed," he adds to his father's comment.

"And I have wronged him on more than one occasion."

"You think that for this he will forgive you and return you to his bountiful bosom?" Galahaut sounds more than a little doubtful.

344

"If I do this with that as my intention, then even if I succeed to finally win his love and respect, then it will have cost me my own."

Erik turns to his father, as if to ask if the older man can make any sense of this discourse.

"That is the motivation of a true knight." Even not understanding, Erik is now convinced by the sincerity of his God-Father.

"God speed my brother, and may the virgin look after your soul."

Lancelot bows and leaves the father and son.

Likely, he will never, ever see them again.

Faron impatiently follows Lancelot through his last preparations to leave. His full focus being on assuring himself that he has all his necessary equipment, ready and available.

There is no space at present, to direct him to reflect on the events leading up to this moment. So the ghost in the shell, just has to do his best to be patient, and wait.

It is only after he is aboard the boat taking him back to the mainland, that Faron can quieten his mind enough to find out what has happened.

One of Galahaut's men had appeared with information that a small fleet of Viking ships had been seen off the coast of Scotland.

And local sailors had heard that they were bound for Portshead.

From there, they were to leave the ships and wait for a Scottish and Viking army coming down from the North.

They were to come a little in advance, just in case there were heavy storms crossing from the Kingdom of Norway, and they would need an extra day or two before they could meet up.

Then they would attack Camelot from the sea, while the army would capture the land.

Angelique, on hearing this, immediately prepared to leave Sorelais so as to warn her father.

Erik had planned to ride with her but was blocked by Galahaut who believed that Arthur would imprison him for his part in the theft of the sceptre.

So the princess, with her two servants, set off alone.

It was then discovered that the soldier was in fact, under a spell of Morgan Le Fey, and that the message, although mainly true, was only part of the plan.

Arthur was sure to ride out to ambush the Vikings once they left their ships.

Only, there would already be a small part of Mordred's army arrived before the ships.

They would be to hide in a small forest, not far from the coast, until Arthur had passed towards the shore.

They would then circle him and his knights and block them from retreating.

The Vikings were to stay on their boats, until signalled to disembark, fighting.

The king would have nowhere to run or to hide.

He could only wait until Mordred himself would arrive with his full army and crush the old king.

And this is the reason that the crazy knight is riding to his own doom.

Ch. 56 The Table of War

Al is on his last stop before reaching the point where Arthur and his small army of knights and soldiers are blocked by Mordred's men.

He is now in a tavern, less than a day's ride from the multiple camps.

Things had evolved somewhat since his contact with Lancelot just before leaving Galahaut's castle.

He has just been in contact with the body of Lancelot, and is contemplating both his evening meal, and the current situation.

Lancelot is also trapped, also pinned down by Mordred's troops.

But then again, there are not enough of the enemy troops to attack either Arthur or Lancelot, without the other being freed to enter into the battle.

He looks down at his plate. The pool of gravy represents the sea, on which some bits of bread float the Viking ships.

Along the edge of the gravy Arthur's meat scraps are encircled by a troop of enemy soldiers, in the form of potatoes.

Behind the potatoes is the small forest of peas, where Mordred's troops were hidden but are now trapped Lancelot and company.

And circling the forest is more bread, which is to say, Mordred himself and his personal soldiers and knights.

The forest is not attackable, but the knight cannot dare to challenge the much stronger forces against him.

Arthur has built defences against the Viking ships, so any attack from there would be only a diversion while the real thrust would come from the shore.

However, the distance between the forest and the shore is not great. So if that army turned its full attention towards those on the beach, they would not be able to defend their backs from those in the forest.

Which means, that for the moment, things are at a stale-mate.

For the moment, being the operative term, as the rest of Mordred's army would be arriving within the next few days.

With hundreds of disposable foot troops, he would not then hesitate to assault the forest.

Not only that, but he would be greatly reinforced by the presence of his aunt, the powerful Morgan Le Fey.

As long as Arthur or Merlin don't have the sceptre in-hand they and their allies would be defenceless against any magical attack.

Of course, Arthur has his army at Camelot, but they had been instructed to wait for his personal orders before moving out of the walled city.

This would be so not to leave it unprotected, in the case that Mordred would take that opportunity to take over his castle, and, in passing, capture the Queen Guinevere.

Al, feeling tired and despondent drags himself up to bed, but cannot sleep.

For nothing better to do, he reminds himself of the last time that he projected himself into Lancelot's body, only a few hours earlier...

The wind is in his face, it tunnels his hair behind, the thrill and excitement pump through his body.

Speed, danger, excitement.

This is the real Lancelot.

Yes, he is likely to be riding towards his death, death and glory.

The countryside flashes by, a kaleidoscope of passing impressions.

Faron is fascinated by the lack of any form of deeper reflection in the hero's mind.

The stereotypical Viking warrior, or Startrek Klingon, come to mind, where an honourable death that future generations will remember in songs of valour is the highest accolade, and desire.

A crazy, bloodlust, battle scenario fills all of Lancelot's consciousness and fantasy.

'This is so insane, how can one plan to dive into such field of Hellfire without any care or consideration for one's own safety or wellbeing?

I'm sure that I won't be in this body when he's getting himself chopped up like some medieval salami, by some drunken, handicapped, one-eyed butcher.'

And yet, maybe not.

The forever selfish, self-protecting, Faron is having an inner conflict.

Exactly what would it feel like to offer himself, body and soul, literally, for the sake of someone else?

To put an ideal, a belief, a person, a principle over and above his own immediate comfort and well-being.

351

A vague memory of one of his therapists drifts back into mind.

They are in a modern office.

The young therapist is leaning back onto his black leather and steel armchair, (the exact same model as his own, must reinforce the feeling of equality).

"James, (he clearly has problems with Pierre-Alain), you might do well to try and move your perspective away from your victim consciousness.

As long as you feel the need to protect yourself from your perceived attacks from everyone else, you will never be in a position to give of yourself to others.

For, it is only when we can really give that we can open to fully receive."

He had reasonably considered this to be total crap at the time.

However, something, somewhere within himself, within the muscled carcass of this idiot knight is forcing him to reconsider.

His thoughts drift to another idiot knight; 'The Ingenious Nobleman Sir Quixote of La Mancha'.

He starts to hum, and then to sing …

"To dream ... the impossible dream ...
To fight ... the unbeatable foe ...
To bear ... with unbearable sorrow ...
To run ... where the brave dare not go ...
To right ... the unrightable wrong ...
To love ... pure and chaste from afar ...
To try ... when your arms are too weary ...
To reach ... the unreachable star ...

This is my quest, to follow that star ...
No matter how hopeless, no matter how far ...
To fight for the right, without question or pause ...
To be willing to march into Hell, for a Heavenly cause ."

Lancelot must have gotten a speck of dust in his eyes, as it seems that he might be crying.

The rational part of Faron's mind is screaming against this new entrance into insanity, but it is too late.

Pride and Esteem, are potent forces.

"Into the valley of death rode the six hundred…
            Theirs not to make reply,
                    Theirs not to reason why,
                            Theirs but to do and die."

A wave of insane happiness curses through the broken man's soul, healing, in one magical, unreasonable, impossible moment, years and years of subjugation and self-doubt.

"And what is more, you'll be a man, my son."

There they are, Mordred's troops, appearing from out of the little forest, just as he was informed that they would.

The plan is to attack, creating as much noise and confusion as possible.

So giving Arthur some time to respond and protect himself.

"For God and King!" He screams and charges headlong into the advancing troops.

The adversaries turn towards the crazy horseman. Their reactions are satisfyingly strong.

They start to regroup to confront the lone challenger.

Faron is having trouble breathing. His heart is belting out a heavy rock rhythm, his lungs are pumping out mini, 'ha's', 'ha-ha-ha-ha' and he is as wired as after having hit two long lines of coke.

And yet, he is feeling as relaxed as if he just had a long session of slow sex and is now mellowing out with a sweet joint.

Not that there is time to reflect, he is about to make his first contact with the line of horsemen.

What is fundamentally different between mounted cavalry and foot solders is that, on foot, you meet your foe, and stay and fight with him until one of you is beaten, or runs away.

When on horseback, you charge through the ranks, in general, not stopping until you have passed all the way through to a clear point where you might turn, and then charge in the other direction.

Hence, it is not until they have finished their first pass and have turned that they realise that the reaction of the other army was not solely due to his appearing.

Behind him there is a battle raging.
Behind him there would have to be others fighting against the troops.
Behind him there has to be …

Galahaut.

Now there will be a battle.
Now there will be victory
Now there will be a saved king, and peace between him and Arthur.

Now there is a battle horn!

He turns on his saddle, just in time to see the form of another army bearing down on them.

If Arthur would have been warned and had mounted an attack to reinforce this action, they would have been able to break through the line and join him.

But now, with reinforcements on their way, it has become impossible.

"Retreat! Retreat!" He screams at his friend and his knights. "Reinforcements are coming, we'll be surrounded."

"The forest!" Galahaut commands his men, who turn and follow their leader towards the safety of the trees.

In an instant they have found the protection of the woods.

Protected, but imprisoned. The other army, an advanced section, led by Mordred himself, has already encircled the forest.

So here they now are, blocked.

As long as they keep them surrounded, Mordred does not have the necessary troops to assail Arthur's now fortified camp, nor to capture Lancelot and Galahaut in the trees.

By the same logic, neither of the true kings can escape, while the pretender controls the paths.

And so, for the moment, all there is to do, is to wait, and see what the future will bring.

Ch. 57 Weaving

Al wakes, refreshed from a good night's sleep, his mood has strangely improved.

Is this due to Faron's new perspective on life, death and honour or simply the mind and body's ability to re-resource itself with sleep, is anyone's guess.

He returns to his place of the previous evening and prepares to partake of his morning meal.

When, to his surprise and pleasure, he watches as a little grey rat scampers onto the table, and up to his plate.

"Good morning, your wizardry, and would you care to join me for some breakfast?"

The rat, in response, climbs onto its hind legs and wriggles its nose.

"Well, we have biscuits, cheese and a piece of ham." And he proceeds to dissect the afore mentioned foods into rat bite sized morsels.

However, the rat does not eat the food as offered, it scampers round his plate, moving the bits into a specific order.

This order creates words, and the words read; '*bring food*'.

It doesn't take Al more than a few moments to realise that Arthur's army has been in a state of siege for several days now. They had hurried to intercept the Vikings from landing, they would not have taken more than minimum rations.

"Food, I'll buy as much as I can carry." And, message passed, the rat dives into the cheese and ham, the bread can be for the mice.

After finishing up, he goes and orders as much food and drink as the feels that his horse can carry.

He then hurries off to a local tanner and has himself made the first over leather rucksack.

It has a large pouch to carry bread, which although voluminous and filling, is relatively light. And a deep side pocket, in which to hide and protect the sceptre.

He then rushes back to the inn to pack the rest of the food and drink, and his personal affairs on the back of his horse.

Quite soon after, he and Merlin the rat are on their way to meet up with Arthur.

Exactly how he is going to weave his way through the two columns of Mordred's army, is yet to be seen, but all that is important, for the moment, is that he is on his way.

As there could be no military advantage to control the coastline, Al is quite confident that the opposing army will not bother to waste any personnel on the seaward path.

And so, in spite of the near impossible nature of his commission to deliver both the sceptre and a horse full of provisions to Arthur and his camp, he is more than relaxed.

Which is not the best attitude to have when an enormous white-tailed sea eagle suddenly shoots up from the cliffs underneath you.

The horse bolts and runs like crazy along the narrow hilltop path.

The bird circles inland and swoops down heading directly to collide with them, below, only the crashing waves against the hard-black rocks.

Al tries to slow his horse, but it will have none of it.

The eagle is only yards away and will definitely hit them full on.

Blinking in thought, Al grabs the length of one of the reins, and in the very last moment, violently smacks the horse on the flank.

The pain and shock have the effect of an electric jolt and the poor creature bounds forward with a mighty leap.

Al bends forward hugging the horses neck and bending his own down and behind it.

The eagle, advancing at full speed, cannot correct its trajectory enough and barely touches his back with her claws.

The new leather backpack now has a long gash across its length, but otherwise, for the moment, they are without further damage.

But surely not for long.

The eagle climbs using the sea thermals to boost it up, and makes a long, gliding turn.

It passes over them keeping its altitude.

The first attempt failed, however, there is no cover, and no reason why the second sweep will not succeed to send them to a painful end.

The choice of where to attack has been well planned out, the path is along the cliff-face, there is no way to climb off the path and back onto the rest of the land.

And yes, it is clearly an attack, and even not being able to see the colour of the bird's eyes, they are surely yellow, and looking through them, can be no other person than the witch, Morgan Le Fey!

There seems to be another object in the sky, but it is much too high and far away to be sure to be anything.

Al has no more ideas as what to do. His horse has tired itself out and has stopped running. It also seems to have realised that there is really nowhere to run.

Could he possibly get it to lie down on this narrow ledge? It seems pretty much impossible as an idea, but as there's nothing else to try, he slides off the horse's back.

Pulling the inner rein downwards and applying pressure to what most people would wrongly term as the horse's knee, he attempts to get it kneel down.

It knows that there is not really enough room and it is starting to resist.

Al knows that if the horse panics, they will both definitely end up in the wash.

Almost by instinct he looks across.

And there it is.

Swooping down like a second world war bomber, it is not going to miss this time.

'Three hundred feet captain. Coming in for the final run. Ready the bombs. There'll be nothing left when we've finished here.'

He gives up on the horse and hides himself against the rock face.

Too late, he realises that his sword is safely lashed onto his saddle, there is no way to release it in time.

Nothing to defend himself with other than a short blade.

First his horse and then a direct attack on him.

Even if he could climb back onto the land, the eagle is almost big enough to carry him off. And even if it couldn't, it would still surely kill him.

In total fear and fascination, he peeks over the top of the ridge, it must be almost upon them.

It is so close that he can see the yellow, magically controlled eyes.

It is only seconds away when he notices a huge missile plummeting towards the earth.

No, not towards the earth, towards the eagle.

They hit with a bone-breaking thud.

The second eagle's momentum, (yes, another eagle), has taken them both, hard onto the ground.

They must both be very hurt and in quite some pain.

The white-tail moves to attack the other, a golden eagle, but the movement is very ungainly, the wing must be broken.

It tries once or twice more, then seems to spit at the other, before giving up and turning away.

All the energy has left it, and it is only interested in nursing its damaged member.

The golden turns its head towards the boy and seems to wink its eye before losing its focus on them and then, it too, heading off as best it can.

Not to skit his horse more, he walks her the rest of the distance of the ledge before remounting.

He is now high above the shoreline and can make out Arthur's camp along the beach.

He can also clearly identify the small forest where Lancelot and Galahaut are holed up.

In between the two friendly camps, there is an impressive line of Mordred's soldiers.

And, just off the shore, there are three Viking galleys.

Al has come to a full stop. He has absolutely no idea what to do.

Faron, looking on like some pervert voyeur is keeping himself away from the boy's consciousness, hoping that he will come up with something.

Just then, they feel something moving around in their tunic.

It is the rat.

Merlin must have temporarily 'vacated' the little rodent body and gone off to try and find something to neutralise Morgan with.

'Bloody successfully', Faron acknowledges to himself.

Now that the danger has passed, he has now returned to their, 'little helper'.

The rat jumps out his shirt, scampers down his trousers and onto the grass.

'What now, little wizard?'

It then starts to run down the track.

The track that leads directly to the enemy army's encampment.

It almost seems that he can hear Al muttering to himself, 'you can't be serious.'

And then, someone shrugs their shoulders, and they continue walking.

Being quite high up and far away, they are not likely to be spotted for quite some time.

They continue on for some time without incident.

From their vantage point they can see both the shore and the sea.

Something is happening in the sea.

There seems to be a wind rising, but only in one spot.

It is frothing up the water and creating some type of mist.

It must be just the droplets of water, thousands of them.

The water-fog is getting stronger and covering more and more of the surface.

Whether it is Faron or Al that realises what is going on first, one will never know.

What is clear is that this is the work of Merlin, and it is their passage through the camp.

By the time that they reach the edge of the tents, there is an awful storm, wind and fine rain.

The generated mist is so thick, that it is difficult to see even a few feet in front.

That is, for everyone else but Al.

He has no difficulty what-so-ever. He is protected by an invisible barrier, that feels to Faron like a science-fiction, force field.

They weave their way between the tents and the soldiers.

The troops are so caught up with trying to hold onto their equipment and tie the tents down, that seem not to see the boy and his horse, not at all.

Ten minutes after entering the encampment they are out the other side, and it only takes another few minutes before Al is explaining to the sentry who he is and why he is there.

Fortunately, an old, bearded figure looms up out of the darkness and opens the passage.

“Thanks,” is all that Al can think to say.

“You’re very welcome,” responds the smiling wizard.

Ch. 58 The Calm Before the Storm

They are in Merlin's tent.

Faron is exhausted, having succeeded to bring the stuff that the wizard has asked for, and managed to get through the enemy lines, he can think of nothing else but getting some sleep.

"You can go to sleep now, but you will need to awake before dawn. You will have to pass back through Mordred's camp, and early in the morning, they will be less attentive.

For the moment your face is not known to them, but that will not last for long, so you will need to benefit from that this time."

He got in, he'll get out again. He knows that he doesn't have much choice.

"Good luck and God speed."

Faron sighs and heads off to bed.

He is having trouble getting to sleep. The latest news from Merlin was more than troubling.

Although Mordred's main army had met with an unexpected and quite powerful adversary.

Unexpected for them, that is to say.

Unfortunately; while the foot soldiers held the new foe at bay, the mounted corps abandoned the main convey, and headed down to meet with their king.

The good news was that the main mass of the army might never arrive, the bad news is that 'the cavalry' would arrive very soon.

Arthur was suitably concerned with this turn of events, preferring to immediately turn his attention inland, ignoring the likely arrival of the Vikings, and charge for the forest.

Once shielded by the relative protection of the trees, to then try find a means to contact his own army at Camelot and have them come to rescue him.

However, so it seems, Merlin had counselled him to wait a little longer as he had a possible plan.

That he wouldn't even share his project with his king, just went to prove how very paranoid he was becoming, in his old age.

The king acquiesced, and he too went to bed.

The next day, Faron passed from body to body, keeping track, as best he could, all that was happening from the different points of view.

Both Al and Lancelot were tense, as were both their camps.

Everyone wanted to act, but Faron knew that now wasn't yet the moment, so he did the best that could to keep everyone calm.

The day passed slowly, both beside the water and within the trees.

The two allied armies could easily see each other, but the mass of enemy troops made any other contact impossible.

Of course, there were some that, sly as a fox, knew how to pass through that enemy, as if they weren't even there.

Then again, they also had a magician to hide their back.

The day finally passed into night, and they did their best to get a good night's sleep.

Tomorrow will be quite another day.

Ch. 59 The Storm

They were up before the sun.

Arthur's men had been covertly removing the temporary blockades that they had put into place.

Faron, unknown to anyone else, had kept a close liaison between Arthur and Lancelot.

He was under the impression that it was thanks to some manipulation of Merlin's.

The wizard, although not understanding how Faron was managing it, was ready to take the praise, and to ask no questions.

The fact that he believed that Al and Lancelot could, somehow communicate, was due to his conviction that the two were linked in ways that were beyond his ken.

The king was ready, his troops were ready, Al, at his side was ready.

They could not afford to wait; the opposing sentries would surely notice and prepare.

Arthur looks to Al, Al nods his head, the King silently signals the attack.

At exactly the same moment, Lancelot nods to Galahaut, and he too signals the attack.

The unthinkable is happening, Arthur has chosen to start the battle.

However, the unthinkable is only unthinkable to those that haven't already thought about it, yet.

This attack had been anticipated for some time, and Arthur's preparations had not gone unnoticed.

What Mordred's army had not counted on, however, was the simultaneous charge coming from behind them.

It was not possible to have been aware of their preparations for this morning's ride.

They had the whole of the forest surrounded, and they were keeping careful watch on Arthur's encampment, so there was no way for any information to have passed between the two camps.

And although there were lookouts posted, there were also distracted by the battle against Arthur that the rest of the troops were preparing for.

The first onslaught was to be confronted by two solid rows of archers and lance-men.

But suddenly, there was an unaccountable gust of hot wind, sucking a mass of fine sand across from the beach and showering the soldiers with a rain of burning particles.

The king's men erupted from behind the blistering, yellow-gold blanket.

The archers, well trained as they were, almost automatically, let loose their projectiles.

The rain of arrows had some success, but the shock of the onslaught had bought a moment of confusion, and the knights had already broken through the ranks.

The heavy, sharpened swords, cutting a swath of blood and pain as they pass.

Al had been instructed to wait until the first wave had passed before putting himself into danger.

Faron can feel the unique mixture of fear and excitement filling his young frame.

Having shared in this quite same experience through Lancelot's body, he knows it well.

The thought of the knight, immediately transports him into the other's body.

He is charging the weak line of soldiers that were supposed to block this from happening.

Faron can taste and smell the man's blood-lust.

His heavy sword seems as light as a length of rope.

The strong, supple wrist, spins the shining spitter of death.

The feeling is heady and exhilarating.

Higher calm, yet totally wired.

Again, as if one could combine the effects of a mega-joint and two long lines of coke.

Lancelot rises himself on his stirrups, looking for the king.

The king, and behind Arthur, there is Al…

Al crashes through what remains of the archers and lance holders,

His sword is much shorter and lighter than that of his master. He still has neither the physical strength nor the practice to wield a full size, full weight weapon.

A soldier attacks, his short sword threatening to slide up Al's left side, under his heavy, leather, fighting tunic, and under his ribcage.

The time to lift his sword up and over the horse's body would take too long.

He slips his left foot out of the stirrup, and kicks at the other's sword arm.

Catching him on the elbow, the arm shoots across towards the horse's head, twisting the soldier away from Al.

He now bends across the beast's body, and hammers the guy, heavily on the head with the hilt of his sword. He falls and is likely to be trampled to death by one of horses behind.

He hears several loud 'wooshes', bright lights and heat on one side of his face.

He turns to see the cause of this, and is almost blinded by three massive torches that have just been lit.

The Vikings have just been invited to the party.

But Al has no time to worry about the savage, sea faring warriors sailing towards the shore and their unprotected backs.

He has enough to do to protect himself.

A pick is heading towards his head. A semi-acrobatic pivot to left and lean back onto the cushioned saddle, and it passes harmlessly into the air.

Then quickly bend back, swipe with sword, and a permanent stomach ache for his would-be killer.

The noise is deafening, the activity is omnipresent, the intensity is electric.

Faron, in his real life, who has only ever fought when drunk, is feeling ecstatic.

He knows that his bodies, both Al and Lancelot are sustaining cuts and bruises, there must be pain, they must be suffering.

But nothing counts for anything, all there is, is the pell-mell thrusting, stabbing, slicing, and screaming.

Yes, there is screaming, much screaming, and quite a lot of this screaming is coming out of his own mouth.

And in the greatest craziness and danger that he has ever experienced, he finds …, peace.

He is back in Findhorn, in the Universal Hall, during the Inner Peace, cathartic workshop.

Everyone is screaming out their pain and life suffering. Some are crying in anger, some are crying in pain, some are crying softly, some cry in silence, rocking themselves in some autistic, session invoked psychic break.

Faron screams and screams, but never releases himself to his deep, inner demons.

He is going through the motions, as with every other attempt to contact and release his buried pain.

Here, here on the battlefield, there is no make believe. Here he is one hundred percent present and implicated.

This is his reality.

To the surprise of those close by, almost simultaneously, both Lancelot and Al scream, at the very top of their lungs.

"I am Faron, Pierre-Alain James Ferguson and I exist!"

Then comes the anger and the hate.

Slash, cut, hit, scream.

Years and years of pent up rage erupt from his mountain prison.

"Fuck you! Fuck you! Fuck you!"

Lancelot is trying to control this overpowering need to cut and to kill. His target is not to decimate the other army, only to get to Arthur and create a human, horse corridor for the king and his knights to gain the safety of the woods.

Only this is not to be.

"Lancelot, behind you!" Galahaut calls out a warning.

A squadron of arrows is raining towards them.

The knight twists his shield up and behind to protect his head and neck.

The woods behind, now vacated by their forces, have been infiltrated by the enemy and archers have benefitted of the trees to gain altitude.

"To the beach," responds the White Knight, and continues to head towards his king.

He hacks a path to the king's followers.

"Arthur, the woods are overrun, we must return to the beach, there is no choice."

It is clear that this is not an option that he wishes to accept.

Only, a second wave of Mordred's troops are appearing from both sides of the forest.

His mounted troops have arrived, and Arthur is now totally outnumbered.

"Retreat! Retreat!" He turns his horse back towards the sea, only to return to the prison that he has been blocked in, these last few days.

Fortunately, there are few of the enemy's troops to slow them down and they soon are arriving on the sandy ground.

But what of the Vikings?

There is a storm at sea, but only at sea.

The wind is howling, the waves are crashing and there is a fog hanging over the waters.

However, there is also a strong wind blowing down from the North, that is starting to dissipate the fog, and somehow calm the sea.

Merlin, back to the fighting is involved with his own personal battle.

He has succeeded to stall the ships, but now, another magical force is working to neutralise his efforts.

Although Morgan Le Fey, cannot use her powers against Arthur or his physically close allies, nothing stops her attacking Merlin's spells against her own supporters.

The day is drawing to a close, and in the weird medieval system of things, the fighting for the day has come to an end.

Merlin allows the storm to pass, and returns, exhausted to the centre of the camp.

"They were prepared for us, there must a traitor in our midst." Grumbles Lancelot.

"Obviously," Merlin does not seem particularly perturbed by this remark.

"You have nothing more to say on this?" Galahaut supports his friend.

"She is capable to take over the body of almost anyone of a weak personality. There are many in any group that would not succeed to protect themselves against her powerful influence."

"And you choose to do nothing about this?"

"Merlin has my total trust," the king turns to erstwhile enemy. "But tell me, Galahaut, why, after you that has passed between us these last months, why are you here? Why should you risk your life to protect someone that has wronged you so, as I have done?"

"It is neither for nor against you that I am here. Lancelot is my soul brother, I would not let him die alone, I would'st be at his side."

"For what ever reason, I thank you and your men for the sacrifice that you have made, but I cannot allow you to die for me.

I will attempt to talk with my nephew and beg him to allow you to leave.

You are not part of this war."

"I will not leave my brother but thank you for the offer. If my men might have free passage that would greatly lighten my soul and aid my passage to the next life."

"So be it. Now you," he turns to the knight, "why in God's name are you returned?"

Faron smiles.

"Because, just as Galahaut is my brother, you are my father. And even if father and son argue, they are still family.

You brought me into your household, and I have disrespected your generosity.

For such, I have been punished, and rightly so.

However, my disgrace is no excuse for not returning in time of need and offering, once again, my sword and my allegiance to my king."

And so saying, he draws his sword and offers it to Arthur.

Arthur hesitates for a moment before accepting the symbolic weapon.

"You are a complicated piece of work, Lancelot of the Lake. I still hate you for what you have done.

And yet, you have, without hesitation, on more than one occasion put your life in danger to support your king.

I cannot, nor will not forget your errors, but will gladly forgive them. Just as any father, will always forgive his prodigal son. Come."

He takes Faron by the arms and brings him to his feet.

"I am proud of my son."

He looks deeply into the eyes of his father, to finally see that which he has sought, all of his life, respect.

So not to shame Lancelot with his uncontrollable emotions, he seeks the relative calm of the body and psyche of Al.

However, Al is not untouched by the scene either. Fortunately, he can easily melt into the background.

He seeks out his sleeping sack, and beds down for what might very well be, his last night on this earth.

Ch. 60 Le Morte D'Arthur

The morning is bright and cheerful.

The bright, yellow sun has already passed the horizon.

The soldiers are finishing the very last of their supplies.

There is no point in saving anything, there will be no supper tonight.

A herald calls then to attention.

Mordred wishes to talk to them.

Arthur walks stiffly to the barricade.

Mordred is waiting for him some feet from the other side.

"Good morning, uncle."

"Good morning Mordred."

"We should talk."

"I am here to listen."

"You are totally surrounded. The Vikings are ready to land, and I have ten times as many men than you have."

"So what do you suggest?"

"I suggest that you cede to me, uncle.

That you offer to me both your throne and your allegiance."

"And for such an act?"

"Any man that will accept me as his regent will be spared."

"And the others?"

"On their own heads, be it." He smiles at his own humour.

"And if I do not bend before you?"

"Then they will all die."

"I will not have the deaths of these good men on my conscience, so," he sighs wearily, "I …"

"…must refuse."

He turns surprised at this intervention.

"Lancelot, it is not your place."

"Of course, your Majesty, only, maybe one might well to look over yonder, before making any decisions."

They all look over to where the knight is indicating.

Behind the forest, the land rises quite sharply. On the ridge, to the right one can easily make out a large body of men.

And, using his spyglass, Arthur can easily make out, his own standard.

"Cousin," he politely passes the farsight over to his adversary.

"But, but, it's not possible. They would never leave Camelot without your personal order."

"And while you might reflect on the impossible," Lancelot gestures to the other side of the woods.

Here, there is another troop of cavalry. Shining brightly, is the armour of a shiny copper hue.

"Maybe we should wait to surrender until all the players have had the chance to throw their dice."

Arthur, retrieves his spyglass, turns, without saying a word and returns to the camp.

One might well have expected that Mordred, seeing that he was now outnumbered, would have gathered his troops and tried to orchestrate some sort of a get-away.

It is what any rational and sane leader would have done.

Only,

… he isn't.

Only minutes after Arthur has returned to the fire, the alarm sounds.

It does not last long, as it is difficult to blow a warning after having your throat slit.

Mordred's men force themselves through the lines of Arthur's men.

The knights circle the two kings, they will die before any royal blood can be split.

It doesn't take long before they are totally surrounded.

Faron is now facing death through the eyes of both Lancelot and Al.

The knight seems strangely resigned, his only thoughts are to fight as long as he is capable to and die a noble death.

Al is genuinely scared. The heat of the battle of yesterday has worn off, leaving him wounded and exhausted. Now, all that is left is the fear of the pain and hoping that it will be a quick and relatively painless deliverance.

Knowing that he cannot really die, and in something like a video game scenario, once he dies, he will just have to start this level again, he is also most interested in a quick and sudden death.

However, making the choice to rest in Lancelot's body, would not have been the one that he would have chosen earlier on in his real life.

Of course, if he would have thought it through, he would have realised that he had other, more reasonable options.

Or maybe he just wanted to hang around and watch how it played out .

"Stop!" The pretender appears from out of the mass.

"Arthur, I will have your crown, your lands and your queen.

These will be rightfully mine."

"Will they?" The king pushes his way through his protectors.

"They will after I have bested you in combat."

"Wait," it is Merlin that comes forward. "Have you forgotten that since the time you last met in battle, your lives are now joined? If one of you should die, then the other will also perish."

"I have no interest in killing my uncle, I just need to best him in a fair fight."

"And that is what you seek, one to one with me?"

"Do you dare to face me, old man?"

Not only is he now quite old, but also tired and wounded from yesterday's battle

"Clear the space, it is time to teach my young nephew a thing or two about manners."

Like at some sort of friendly wrestling match, the soldiers of both camps spread themselves out to form a wide circle around the two opposing monarchs.

They draw their swords.

Arthur stays out of the centre, Mordred advances.

Arthur waits, patiently. His sword, held in both hands, pointing towards the ground.

Mordred, an angry cat, dances on his hind legs, spitting and scratching the ground.

He looks, momentarily away. Faron has seen this move before, but doesn't have the time, nor maybe the inclination, to call out.

'Look away, dive into the attack.'

Which is exactly what he has planned to do.

He dives at the old king.

But age and experience add in this type of combat.

Arthur spins up his sword and squarely blocks the blow to his head.

It is deftly done. The attack is easily thwarted.

However, even this first blow is not without consequence for the old king. There is an obvious 'bend' as he absorbs the impact.

Mordred smiles to himself.

He knows that he is young, fitter, and quicker.

Time, in every sense, is on his side.

What does he care if Arthur's reinforcements arrive, he will have bested the king? He will then have acquired them as his rightful privilege. They will become, his.

And so the combat continues.

Arthur does not attack, he is content to rest on the defensive.

Waiting for Mordred to make mistakes, waiting for opportunities, waiting to win.

And so it seems his strategy might succeed, or it would have, if he would have been fighting an honourable opponent.

Mordred is circling Arthur, the crowd has pulled back to give him room.

Suddenly he gives a cry and rushes his uncle. He moves to place a straight jab, but just as Arthur swings a parry the attack, Mordred spins round him.

The defensive swing takes several seconds, but the attacker has already arrived behind his back.

And, without giving him any chance to turn, appears from his belt, a short, sharp throwing knife.

It enters between the leather jerkin and heavy pants.

They move to intervene but there are too many of his men, they have no chance.

Arthur twists to grab the tiny, stinging insect.

He manages to pull it out.

But he is already well weakened.

Mordred drops his sword and uses all his strength to launch a powerful kick in Arthur's stomach.

He doubles over, and releases Excalibur.

Mordred takes the opportunity to kick the enchanted sword several feet away.

He then circles Arthur and thumps him heavily on the back of the neck.

Arthur sprawls to the ground.

Mordred has disappeared from his sight.

His sword is not so far away, if he could just stretch out his arm, he can surely reach it.

Behind, and overhead, Mordred rises the axe.

It is all as he has planned it.

A one-armed, ex-monarch will never need be considered as a threat.

"Noooo!" Lancelot, in one fluid motion unsheathes his sword and hurls it directly at Mordred.

No-one has time to react.

Least of all Mordred, savouring his ultimate moment of victory.

Now, the ultimate moment of his life.

The sword passes straight through his leather chest-piece, piercing bone and sinew, only for the point to appear out of the back.

Time, as often happens, slows down to a point of relative inertia.

The axe spins beautifully in the air.

Mordred's eyes open in total surprise.

He crumples down to his knees.

His hands cup the shaft of the sword.

The silence and gesture mimic a moment of prayer.

In symmetry, some of his soldiers follow him onto their knees.

The Christians, cross themselves.

"You have killed me."

"I have killed my father," Lancelot rushes to Arthur's side.

"I am sorry, I have again failed you. Can you ever forgive me, my Lord?" Tears welling up before his eyes.

Arthur turns himself over and lays on his back.

"Come here, come close." Only Lancelot, which is also to say, Faron, can hear his last words.

"Sooner or later he would have bested me. I could not, nor would not kill him.

You have performed an important act that has saved all of England.

I am still proud to call you my son.

Now, one last and most important act.

Take Excalibur and throw it out to sea."

"But it will be lost."

"Fear not. It is to be so.

Promise that you will do this thing."

"On my honour."

"Good, now I might die in peace."

Arthur gives a half smile, takes a long, last breath, and dies.

Ch. 61 After the Storm

Lancelot looks round for the emblematic sword.

It is not that difficult to locate.

He bends down to get it.

His whole attention is focused on the mythical object.

Then he.

Takes the sword.

He looks not at Arthur.

He looks not at the silent crowd.

Head bowed, he turns towards the sea.

The soft breeze picks microscopic particles of spray.

Heading away from the scene of death.

Heading towards the waters.

His face is salty wet.

Faron, feels.

Pain.

"The king is dead …"

She has appeared from somewhere.

He chooses to ignore her.

"You hold the symbol of power."

Faron can feel the heaviness of the man.

"Both kings, of the North and of the South, have perished today."

She continues in a conversational, even chatty tone.

"There needs to be someone to take their places."

He doesn't want to hear her.

He wishes for silence.

He needs silence.

Silence from the cries of anguish.

Silence from his pain.

But she has another, important agenda.

"England and Scotland could now be united under one banner.

All they need is someone to lead them.

They need a hero.”

He carries on his solemn march.

“You have been adopted as Arthur’s son and now heir.

The people would freely accept you.

Arthur’s son, Mordred’s executioner, the bearer of Excalibur.

And, you would have mine and my family’s support.

Power and glory…

And the princess.

Lady Angelique would be yours for the taking.

The adopted son and the blood daughter of the defunct king.

The perfect and legitimate succession.”

The temptress could be talking to a deaf man.

Faron is, … curious.

He clearly notices Lancelot’s reactions to this rather attractive offer.

Especially that of marrying Angelique, or is that more his own?

The story has ended, this is the epilogue.

Arthur is dead, Lancelot has played has role in this epic tragedy.

Faron thinks back to his days on stage, the 'Faron Show'.

The other performers were family, they were close.

The day that the stage went dark, they all left.

They parted in their separate directions.

Some, never to speak again.

It is the just the same.

All is finished

The end

Angelique, Guinevere, Merlin and Morgan, these were just actors in this play, this farce.

He will send the cursed sword to the depths of the sea and be done with it all.

Faron smiles, there is nothing else to prove.

Behind and beyond the deep, aching sadness, there is release.

He no longer has to be this hero.

He has finally succeeded to be, … a man.

Lancelot takes the sword by the hilt.

"Nooo."

Ignoring the anguish of she that has lost all, he takes all his strength and hurls the weapon into the sea.

But, of course, it never enters into the water.

With an impossible ease and grace, Viviane, the Lady of the Lake, breaks through to the surface, and rescues the sword.

Looking at her adopted son, she blows him a kiss, waves, and dives back into the mirrored waters.

* * * * * * *

They are riding North, the knight and his squire.

There is not much to talk about, which gives Faron plenty of time to ruminate on the events of the past days.

He has read and watched his far share of adventure stories, even participated in some role play games, but they were nothing, what-so-ever like this.

Faron is a hero.

And nobody, not even Lancelot or Al even know about it.

In this world, Faron, the real Faron, does not exist.

He is a ghost that can take over and influence certain people.

The only person who knows the real truth is Friar Brendan, the guide.

Yes, he could seek him out, so as to have an audience to appreciate his heroic and brilliant endeavours.

However, as his guide, he must surely already know.

And so, having no-one else to recount his adventures to, he satisfies himself with replaying the last scenes of his personal action movie.

Especially those parts that led up to the two parts of the 'seventh cavalry' that appeared behind Mordred, just before he was about to slaughter all of them.

Of course it was the Copper Knight that had already attacked and pretty much routed Mordred's main army.

And long before it could arrive to back up the siege against Arthur.

It occurred to him, while inhabiting Lancelot's body, imprisoned in the forest, lost for any solution, wondering who might think to come and rescue him.

In a flash, it came to him that the Copper Knight was only some sort of copy of Lancelot, and if he could enter into this knight's body, why not his doppelganger?

From there it was only a matter of wishing it, as with the others, that he succeeded to 'transport' his consciousness.

From there on in, he only had to suggest that Lancelot needed support for the twin to put together his little army and enter into the fray.

The other story, however was much more intricate.

It was while talking with Merlin that the idea came.

The wizard was explaining that there was an army in Camelot, but Arthur had given explicit instructions that he, and only he could give the order for them to leave the castle unprotected and follow him into battle.

"And Arthur is stuck here," reflects the young fox.

"I'm afraid, even if he succeeded to evade the other army, that there are surely spies on this camp.

And Mordred would know almost immediately. and the king would be in great danger of being captured or killed."

Thinking of the situation of the Copper Knight, he then asks

.

"But couldn't you do the same trick that you did to create the Copper Knight?"

"The creation of a double took many, many moons and a great deal of preparation."

Faron has a vision of a scene from Harry Potter.

"And if you took a hair from the king's head and brewed a magic potion, could you not make someone look like the king?"

The magician's face lights up, he even starts to smile.

"Excellent, excellent. Uther Pendragon."

"Who?"

"Do you know nothing boy? Uther Pendragon is King Arthur's biological father."

"Of course," Faron had taken so much of Al's consciousness that the boy's knowledge was largely inaccessible, at that moment.

"I disguised Uther to resemble King Gorlois, so that he might enter into his castle and bed his wife, the Queen, Lady Igraine."

"Excellent. Can you do it again?"

"Yes, no. I will need certain herbs and tinctures from my cabin, but there is no way to get them here." He shakes his head sadly.

"And even if I could get them here, there is still the problem that we can trust no-one.

If any of the knights, no, not even you, were to suddenly disappear, Mordred would be informed and all roads to Camelot watched and defended."

"And if someone could get your supplies, sneak his way through the troops, and get to you without anyone seeing him, would that work?"

"Young man, you have succeeded to work your own miracles, the how, even I cannot fathom, but what you suggest is nigh on impossible."

"But could it work?"

"If, yes if your friend could enter into my house, which is pretty well locked up, steal the right herbs, powders and tinctures, and get himself here, un-detected, I think that I could do the rest."

"Fine, give me the list and how one might recognise them
..."

The Faron, being not only an acrobat, but also a thief had
no problems getting into Merlin's little cottage and
finding the magical ingredients.

Then getting through the enemy camp, well, he just
walked through. Who would think to stop this rough
looking person, who strolls through, as if he owns the
joint?

Al was waiting for him to help him pass into their camp,
but that was easy, he just offered to patrol a part of the
perimeter as his turn of sentry duty.

Seeing Faron enter at one moment, and Arthur leave
some time later was a little unnerving for the youth, but
he had been well prepared for this.

Faron was a little concerned about drinking the formula,
still remembering the description of the taste of the
Polyjuice potion.

However, the 'real' potion, was more like a healthy,
although rather salty, soup.

"Here, put these on," Merlin passes a set of imperial
clothes, to the thief, they are much too big for him.

At least for the moment.

The changing process is not unpleasant.

Arthur is not only plumper but also taller than Faron.

So, apart from the weirdness of watching his stomach grow larger and rounder, the world slightly shrinks.

When he first starts to move, he can feel, at the same time, the immense power of the man, but also the stiffness both of age and of, simply, not being an active acrobat.

"Go," Merlin is impatient that he gets underway. He throws the old, heavy cloak, under which Faron has entered, back over his shoulders, with the hood obscuring his new, noble countenance.

"Good luck," he smiles, and pushes his ersatz monarch out of the tent.

Faron grabs his old, worn, cloth shoulder bag and hurries into the night.

He passes by Al, that gives him a mini-bow, and half smile.

He stops for a moment and lights a pipe, then wanders, almost aimlessly along the limit of Mordred's fortification.

"What you doin' 'ere?"

"What?"

"You crazy? You's outside the perimeter."

" 'ow's I t' know? Where's the barrier?"

"There ain't no barrier."

"By'r Lady. I could've been killed."

And shaking his head, he stomps past the guard, muttering, "Idiots".

Faron is amused and impressed with the ease and confidence that this incarnation has to become quasi-invisible, strolling with total confidence through the rival camp, wearing the form of their arch-enemy.

Surprisingly soon he is leaving the enclosure. There is no challenge exiting from this direction.

He walks for some minutes until he falls across a small campsite.

Around the fire he finds a tall gangly individual, with a ginger mop for hair, facing a smaller, solid bulldog type.

"Oh mi Gaud," the bulldog exclaims as the stranger lowers his hood.

" 'Truth, it is the exact likeness of the king." Adds the other.

"Come on, we's some ridin' to do. Git the horses ready."

And so the motley crew of king and crooks set out for Camelot.

They arrive by mid-morning.

Faron can feel the tension in his body as they approach the walls of the city, but he is now in charge.

Maybe he has not played the role of king before, but Arthur is well known to both Lancelot and to Al.

Further more, this is only one more theatre piece that his father is playing in, and Faron knows his father, certainly well enough to pass.

As he is riding up to the gates, he has a flash of a new-age workshop that he attended many years ago.

One of the exercises was to choose someone that he had a problem with, someone that he knew well, and during the lunch break, act as if you were him, (or her).

Faron had, not surprisingly, chosen his father.

He had discovered two things during the exercise.

One that he didn't like or feel comfortable taking as much space, in every discussion, as his father had the habit of doing.

And two, that it was highly successful, and people appreciated his company more than when he was just being himself.

It was going to be fine.

"Open the gates, your king has returned."

"Sire." And gates swing open.

"Summon the knights, I will converse with them."

Without speaking another word, he drops from his horse, and repairs to his private chambers to toilet and freshen up.

One does not appear in public unwashed, and in dirty attire.

Arthur descends to the table chamber, in which the celebrated round table is to be found.

There are many versions of the history and veracity of the myth of this venerated object, Faron smiles to himself. 'Good of me to have conjured up a big one.'

There are many empty seats, but still there must be between thirty and fifty knights present.

"We have been tricked and manipulated by our enemies.

The supposed invasion by the Vikings was but a trap to capture me and my guard.

It is Mordred that is behind this deception. He has encircled my men, and those of Sir Galahaut, and will soon overrun them and put them all to death.

We will leave a minimum guard here to defend the castle, but the rest of my army will prepare to leave in the hour.”

One of the knights moves to speak, one that Faron does not recognise, so he stops him immediately.

“There is nothing to discuss. I will meet you at the gates. May God be with us.”

Arthur nods a salute to his trusted companions and leaves the chamber.

He heads towards the little dining room, he is now starving.

Riding here, playing this role, it is exhausting. Hopefully some food might help.

A page appears.

“Get me some food a drink. … And, there were two riders that accompanied me here, see that the kitchen offers them anything that they might desire.”

‘Why not? They deserve a perk or two.’

There is a movement behind.

"M'lady."

Guinevere enters into the room.

"You spoke of Sir Galahaut having joined the fray. Why would he do that? And do you have news of Lancelot?"

"It is thanks to Lancelot that Galahaut chose to align with me. And their timely arrival is the only reason that you are not already a widow."

"But why would he do so? After all, we have both ejected him from our lives."

"Lancelot is a true hero. He is not, admittedly the brightest of men, nor has he shown much ability to rein in certain impulses," they sort of smile at each other.

"And yet, he is the most loyal and noblest of my knights."

While expressing this out loud, Faron becomes acutely aware of the difference between human frailty and noble intent.

His whole descent into personal Hell has been paved by his own human frailty, but he has always been aware of his own noble intent.

'I am not a bad person, just a good person, often in a bad place.'

"Lancelot is forgiven. I forgive my son for his errors and his weakness's."

Is it possible to forgive – yourself, like that?

Is it possible to take on the role of the person that you most wish to honour and respect you, and just do it?

Can this Arthur, this J.J. really have the right to forgive Lancelot, to pardon Faron?

Clearly, based on his deep, deep feeling of release and thrill of happiness, it does have some effect.

After all, this Arthur is not real, and J.J. is dead, how else could it possibly happen?

"Thank you, husband. Thank you for this magnanimous gesture. He is deeply a good man."

There are tears in her eyes.

'Am I a good son, too, mother?'

But there is no space to ask such a question, and the food is here.

There is only to eat, to make his final preparations and to lead his men into battle.

King Arthur is taking the army from Camelot, to save the life of … King Arthur.

Ch. 62 The Final Chapter

It is nearly nightfall when they arrive outside of the walled keep.

"Open the gates, it is I Lancelot, returned," he calls out into the darkness.

There is some commotion from within, they can hear people calling out.

"I said, it is Lancelot, Lord of the Joyous Guard that returns." He shouts even louder.

"The joyous guard has again lost its happiness; it is again the Dolorous Guard."

"Who dares to contradict Lancelot of the Lake?"

"I do," they look up to a lone figure on the ramparts. Dressed in an armour of …copper.

Al, knows this scene, it was played out before, exactly the same, … but why?

The great, wooden door creaks, and slowly begins to open. Some moments later, the solitary figure of the knight appears.

He shows no haste nor fear. Then strolls, easily towards the two weary travellers.

"Lancelot, you look tired from your travels." He speaks in a soft, friendly manner, his voice slightly muffled by his helmet, which covers all of his head.

"It is not necessary to hide your countenance, knight. Or is there some other reason that you keep your identity mysterious?"

"Indeed there is, but it is not to be for long time."

"Why are you back? You were defeated, this is now my domain."

"I was never defeated; I just chose to withdraw. And now I am returned."

But it's not true, Lancelot was defeated by the Copper Knight, he was there, he saw it happen.

"But, think as you wish, tomorrow you will have your opportunity to face me in a fair fight."

"Why tomorrow, why not today?"

"Because I refuse to fight you today."

"What scares you?"

"That you are too tired to offer a decent opponent. Come, tonight, you are my guests, and tomorrow you will finally have your chance to better me, if you can."

And with that parting shot, he turns and walks back towards the now fully open door.

Two young squires are walking towards them. They lead them through the great door and into the courtyard.

Maids are waiting to show them their rooms, and then to a small dining room where supper is already served. There are only two places, so they take their seats and eat.

Once finished eating, there is nothing else to do but retire to their respective chambers and go to sleep.

From the moment that the Copper Knight left them, neither has said one solitary word.

Al cannot understand this at all, there is no logic to this charade.

Troubled, he does his best to get to sleep.

And, at some point he must have succeeded, for he is awakened by the crowing of the cock.

He washes and descends the stairs to the small dining room.

They have just finished breakfast, and are lingering over a final cup of ale, when a page enters.

"Sire," he bows to Lancelot, "the Copper Knight will be waiting for you in the courtyard, at your own convenience."

"Then please inform the noble gentleman that I will be with him in the shortest time possible."

The boy, bows, and exits.

"It is about time that I finished this story."

"Sire, this is not the first time that we are playing out this scene." Al dares to express his confusion.

"Although it will surely be the last time." And with that particular reflection, the knight hurries off to make his final preparations before this important challenge.

The morning is still cool when they leave the protection of the building and enter into the great courtyard of the keep.

Al is a little surprised to notice that although last time there was only the other knight, no guard, no pages, no-one else, at all.

This time the place in ringed with soldiers and peasants, it is as full as any first division football game before a decisive match.

The two knights face each other off.

The last time that Lancelot challenged the Copper Knight, he attacked first and often.

This morning his is much more cautious. He allows the other to move, to circle, and even to strike.

He seems so much more cool and balanced.

Faron can feel the change.

They know who the other knight is.

They know that he has all the strength and knowledge of Lancelot.

They know that the last time, it was he the victor.

And yet, they also know, that this time, things will end differently.

Lancelot easily parry's the attack but does not strike in response.

He is calm and rested. He has beaten Mordred's invasion and killed the usurper.

The has saved the life and kingdom of Arthur and Camelot.

He is now a real hero.

He will beat this poor copy of himself.

This other Lancelot has not experienced the same things, these last few months.

He is still only a reflection of who he was.

Who we were and who we are, might be identical, but if we give ourselves the permission and the means to grow, we can become, wildly better.

The crowd seems to be becoming a bit restless, they have been promised a show, but little is happening.

"Are you afeared knight?"

"No."

"Then why do you not attack?"

"Because I do not need to. You have already lost."

"Because you think that you are stronger than me, faster than me, more intelligent?"

"No, none of those things. You see, you have brought all
these people here to witness your winning against me.
That is why you have already lost."

"Explain."

"I do not have to win against you.
I have nothing now to prove.
You have no more right here, this is my keep.
If you think otherwise, then prove it."

Al stands bemused.

The story is repeating itself, but not exactly.

It is now the Copper Knight who must prove himself.

It is now the Copper Knight that is forced to attack.

It is now Lancelot that keeps to a defensive posture.

It is now the Copper Knight that is beginning to tire.

And it is now Lancelot that suddenly explodes into a fury
of cuts and thrusts.

Left, right, high, low, and up, and across, then left, and to
the head.

Closer, closer, and then twist, he turns with his back to
him opponent and moves the sword away.

Then with all his might, he pulls it back, striking the knight in the waist using the pommel as the weapon in something Faron remembers as the German, Mordhau technique.

Lancelot seems as surprised as the Copper Knight, but the effect is powerful and instantaneous.

The shiny, off-yellow, armoured fighter goes down, and stays down.

"It is done. Take him away. No, leave his helm, if he wishes to hide his disgrace, that is to his own honour."

"It is done, the keep is again named, 'the Joyous Guard.' "

The people, satisfied, file out.

At the end, it was quite a good fight, and they didn't really care who would win.

"What now, sire?"

"You will hither-to cease to call me sire."

"Pardon."

"You are no longer my squire."

"What? What have I done to displease you? What have I done wrong."

"Cool, cool. You have done absolutely nothing wrong. Quite the contrary, you have been a hero."

"But I don't understand, if I've done nothing wrong, why would you stop me being your squire."

"Because, Al, I have decided to adopt you."

"What?!"

"There is no-one on this earth that I would be prouder to call my son than you."

Faron looks up to the older man. Thirsty to drink in these words that he has waited his whole life to hear.

"Proud?"

"Don't push it, come here."

And the knight grabs the boy and squeezes the air out of his thin lungs.

Faron almost dies in pleasure.

Now get you to your room and make it your own.

Al rushes up to his new room, correctly directed by his own page.

"This way, sire."

"Thanks, thank you."

In totally ecstasy he flings himself onto his bed.

A sudden and total exhaustion invades him.

Too much excitement, too many emotions.

Tired, tired, tired.

He feels like he could sleep forever.

His eyes, close …

"Pierre-Alain, Pierre-Alain, it's time to wake up."

He knows that voice, but what would Angelique be doing in his bed chamber at Lancelot's keep?

He opens his eyes to find himself in a white, sunny bedroom.

Angelique is bending over him, her hair, as yet unbrushed.

"It's Monday morning, you don't want to keep the whole factory waiting for the 'blessing'.

"Blessing?"

"What have you been injecting? Today is Monday, you, as the Factory Prefect, have the honour and privilege of blessing the factory and all your workers.

Now go and take your bath. And come down soon to kiss the girls before they go to school.

You have responsibilities, so take them seriously."

Faron turns and rubs his face on the white silken sheets, hoping against hope, that this is not a dream that he will wake up from soon.
-

Gentle reader, thank you for purchasing this book and I very much hope that you have enjoyed it.

If so, please help others to make the choice to read this by sharing your views with your friends and writing a review on Amazon.

Thank you,

Kindest regards

Gary

Other works

By

Gary Edward Gedall

Island of Serenity Book 1
The Island of Survival

Pierre-Alain James 'Faron' Ferguson is about to commit suicide, in his suicide note he attempts to understand how he has come to have wrecked not only his own life, but also all of those around him.

Pierre-Alain James 'Faron' Ferguson finds himself in a type of 'no-mans-land', between here and there, he must accept to visit the 7 islands before he will be allowed to continue on to his next steps. The islands are named; Survival, Pleasure, Esteem, Love, Expression, Insight and lastly, the Island of Serenity

The Early Years:
Pierre-Alain James 'Faron' Ferguson is born into a well-to-do household of a factory owner, Scottish father and mother of a noble French family

He, and his younger brother Jay, grow up in a home of two distant but invested parents. Already, the first, small stones of his future problems are being put into place.

The Island of Survival:
Faron finds himself on the first of the seven islands, transformed into a prehistoric human form, he must learn how to interact with the local environment and the early humanoid tribe.

Here, he must reconnect with his instinct of survival.

This is the second chapter of Faron's life history, in which he falls in love, becomes a real cowboy, starts boarding school, finds his two best friends, goes to visit his weird aunt, goes skiing in Switzerland, and continues the relationship that brings him the greatest joy, yet the greatest sorrow in all of his life, but more than that would be telling too much.

FREE: If you have not yet read Book 1, Survival, no worries, I have included a shortened version, so as to introduce you to the story and the main characters.

Island of Serenity Book 3
The Island of Pleasure
Vol 1 Venice

Part 1.

Faron finds himself in a past version of Venice, as the owner of an old but grand hotel that doubles as the meeting place for the wealthy men of the City and the high-class escort girls that live in the establishment.

Faron can do anything that he likes without limitation or cost. Not only can he avail himself of the girls, but can eat and drink, without limit, but never suffer from a hangover, nor gain a gram.

So why has the enigmatic guide brought him here, and will his limitless access to life's offerings really bring him the pleasure that he is destined to experience?

Part 2.

 Faron is transformed into an adolescent tom boy. In this more modern version of Venice, 'he' has just 7 days to be made into a high-class escort girl.

What does this experience and the intrigues of the other persons within his sphere, mean for him, on his continuing quest to understand, and to experience, Pleasure?

425

Faron finds himself in the mystery of a long-ago Japan, in the body of a young, trainee Geisha.

Who is this sad, young man that he must help to find back his pleasure in life?

Why must he hide the identity of his mother, from the rest of the world?

Why was the love of his mother's life, stolen away by her sister, known to all as Madame Butterfly?

What part does the feudal lord of the region have in all this?

And how does Faron finally succeed to find the key to rediscovering pleasure in his life?

In this the 5th book of the series, we watch as Faron grows from an adolescent into a young, driven man.

He begins by escaping to New York, before starting his University career, finding back his two school, best friends, Duncan and Mike.

After graduating, the three find themselves setting up a business, manufacturing, buying and importing goods from Indonesia.

Success seems to be just around the corner, but Faron cannot help himself. Bitterness and betrayal, hound him like a hungry dog.

To destroy, his own best friend, is not an act to take lightly, but take it, he does.

And what of Angelique, and his daughter Aideen? He is still emotionally entangled, but is that a good thing, or a very bad thing?

Only time will tell.

The Knight's Tale

Faron, our anti-hero, finds himself transported into the body of Sir Lancelot, at the court of King Arthur.

He is on the quest to heal his self-esteem, but the knight, although noble and brave, is also a flawed human-being.

One person that avoids emotional conflicts but cannot escape his passion for Guinevere.

The knight has lost his memory, so he cannot remember how or why he has come to this point in his history.

And who is Al, his faithful squire who has helped him steal a magical sceptre from his supposed best friend, King Galahaut?

Follow Lancelot through his tortured romantic journey, in a world of court intrigue, magic and heroism.

'Le Morte D'Arthur

In this second and concluding volume of the Island of Esteem, we follow Al, as he continues to demonstrate to Faron, just what it means to be a hero.

Lancelot still is troubled by his past and present inability to impose himself, in any situation other than battle.

We get to understand how it was that Lancelot was forgiven by Guinevere, and why Arthur accepted to call on his help to retrieve the Uffington sceptre.

And how and why Al, chose and succeeded to steal it.

Also, how and why, he will be motivated to steal it, not just and second, but also a third time.

We follow the magical manipulations of Merlin and Morgan le Fey.

And finally, what happens to Lancelot and Al, before, during and after the final battle between Arthur and Mordred.

Adventures with the Master

Dhargey was a sickly child or so his parents treated him. He was too weak to join the army or work in the fields or even join the monastery as a normal trainee monk.

To explain to the 'Young Master' why he should be accepted into the order with a lightened program, he was forced to accompany the revered old man a little way up the mountain.

As his parents watched him leave; somewhere they felt that they would never see their sickly, fragile boy ever again, somewhere they were totally right.

He was a happy, healthy seven year old until he witnessed the riders, dressed in red and black, destroying his village and murdering his parents; the trauma cut deep into his psyche.

Only the chance meeting with a wandering monk could set him back onto the road towards health and serenity.

Through meditation, initiations, stories, taming wild horses, becoming a monkey, mastering the staff and the sword; the future 'Young Master' prepares to face his greatest demon.

Two men, two journeys, one goal.

The Tales of
Peter the Pixie

Peter the innocent, honest, young pixie, and his friends;
Elli, the, 'much older then she looks', modest but
powerful Fairy, Timothy, the old, trustworthy, Toad and
the, ever so noble, Fire Dragon, are the best of friends.

Together, they experience many wonderful and heart-
warming adventures.

Told in a classical children's story style; Peter and his
friends, meet all kinds of creatures and situations.

As with all children, Peter is often confronted with
experiences that he does not know how best to deal with,
and he often reacts in ways that are not the most
appropriate. Fortunately; with the help of his good
friends, good will and common sense, everything always
turns out for the best.

The Zen approach to Low Impact Training and Sports

A simple method for achieving a healthy body and a healthy mind

Many of us approach our fitness and sports activities in an aggressive and competitive fashion.

And even if we feel that we succeed to break out of our comfort zones and win against ourselves or our opponent, there is an important cost to bear.

This level of violence that we have come to accept, so as to reach our goals is also an aggression against ourselves. By removing this need to 'win at any price', and tuning in with our bodies and emotions, we can achieve an enormous amount, all the while being in harmony with our mind, body and spirit.

The Zen approach to Low Impact Training and Sports, is a new softer approach where you can have the best of all worlds.

Picturing the Mind

Vol 1

A simple model capable to explain the functioning and dysfunctioning of the human psyche.

Introduction to the Field theory of Human Functioning

For the average man and woman in the street, the complex and competing theories and models of the human psyche; its development, functioning and dis-functioning are often unhelpful for their understanding of themselves.

This becomes even more problematic when they find themselves in difficulty, as often, even the mental health professionals, who are experts in their own fields, find themselves at a loss to communicate successfully how and why the patent is unwell and what needs to happen to find or regain a healthy balance.

This opens up the question; 'is it possible to image a simple, single model, accessible to everyone, to explain the development, functioning and dis-functioning of the human psyche?'

One that builds on existing theories and models, benefitting from the mass of experience and research of 'modern western' psychological concepts and ideas, but also integrating traditional visions of the human psyche and modern theories from the physical sciences.

Picturing the Mind, is an attempt to answer to this need.

Picturing the Mind
Vol 2

The second volume following on from the initial concepts
will reflect on such subjects as:
Relationships
Exchanging energy
Heart & Soul
Recuperation
Subjective constructions
An unconscious yes, an unconscious no
Me, myself and everyone else
Circles in circles, the micro level
Circles in circles, the macro level
Intuition
Metaphysical reflections

Picturing the Mind

Vol 3

Will deal with:

Psychopathology

Traditional psychotherapy
&
Alternative therapeutic approaches.